A TASTE OF THE FORBIDDEN

THE HUMMUS SERIES
BOOK TWO

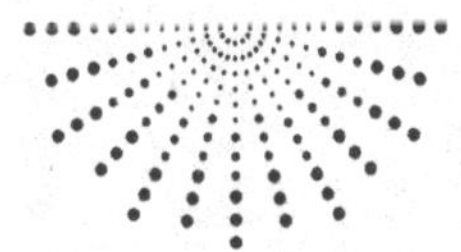

T.K. RICHARDS

First printing, 2021
LNK Publishing
ISBN-13: 978-1-7370438-2-9
www.tkrichards.com

For the Maximus Lovers
He's Back

PROLOGUE

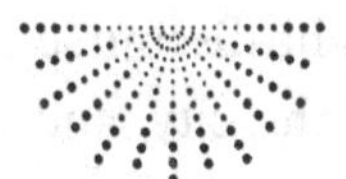

*H*e was warned. Before we eloped in Barcelona, I questioned if it was wise for two people who had not had an argument to get married. We dove into this marriage exceedingly fast with blinders on, and neither of us cared. I was all in for whatever the world of Maximus Sharper flung at me. The spell I was under didn't leave room for the voice of reason, and we were convinced we were destined for each other. Now I bear his last name.

My life changed so dramatically fast, there was no turning back. Two years abroad in the cold and gray land of London, my writing career was still in limbo. Mash's career continued to flourish under new management. He was now an in-demand mixologist, creating countless mixes for A-list artists, and attaching his name to the less established beginners in the industry. Transitioning them from starving to breakout stars.

As a couple we were in sync, but alone I suffered. I felt inadequate without success of my own. In order to fill the void of my lack of accomplishments, I went against my husband's wishes and took an entry level position as a Trainee Negotiator for a real estate firm.

I love beautiful homes, but convincing people to buy them was not my forte.

I learned the business of London's real estate exceptionally fast. It was expensive, the agents were cutthroat competitive, and I needed to be a shark to swim amongst them. In doing so, I missed several of Mash's shows, which was the primary reason he opposed my taking the job in the first place.

My work created a slight discourse in our house, but it helped me learn my way around the city, and introduced me to people I couldn't wait to write about.

Nearly a year after working at the firm, I grew to like working in real estate. That was a mistake. As soon as I got comfortable, my time there ended due to a lack of sales. I cried for a day or two, but with the support of my husband's hefty wallet, I took what I learned and opened a private office as a licensed realtor in the Shoreditch district.

Working for myself meant I controlled my schedule, and could once again travel with my beloved. *I'm sure this is why he was so on board with the idea.* But it was exciting to become an entrepreneur and not feel like dead weight. And as for Shoreditch, I found my tribe. I belonged with the various diverse creatives, artsy folks, colorful streets, and coffee shops, even though I was *posing* as a realtor.

'Nadia M. Sharper' painted in bold white font on the glass of the front door. Sure, I made one sale in three months, but there I was every day, waiting for my second sale to walk through the door to free me from failure yet again.

My back-up plan was more productive as I sat in my plush chair, meant for a fortune five hundred CEO. *Mash went overboard and insisted I have it.* With so much downtime, I used the swanky space as a writing hub away from home. Being surrounded by creatives helped the juices flow with a simple glance outside my office window. Then there was Plan C—buy homes and flip them for a profit.

With business being slow, I closed early one Friday to accompany Mash in Marseille. It was the first weekend we traveled together in a long while, and it felt like it did in the beginning—sweet escapes alongside my personal tour guide, showing me parts of the world, I never imagined I would see.

BRAND NEW ME

I hadn't missed the clouds of cigarette smoke in the clubs, but I did miss seeing Mash come alive onstage, and my guilty pleasure of people watching. After a few peach flavored drinks, I got a little loose and danced provocatively against the railing near the stage. Mash blushed at me grooving solo in my corner, so I simmered down, and fought the urge to move to the beat.

The ambiance of the crowd, the loud sounds of the bass booming from the speaker, and Mash focusing on his work suddenly turned me on. *Oh how I love a working man. Who doesn't?*

I flashed myself with a club flyer to cool down, and shy away my raised nipples piercing through my top. The peach schnapps and vodka also played a role in my sudden yearning to be pillaged by my husband hard at work. I turned away from the crowd until my boobs were no longer on high beam, then returned to face the stage to continue watching the show.

Mash winked at me, and my face flushed. *Dammit, he saw what happened.* To escape the naughty thoughts flashing in my head, I crowd surfed the faces from the atrium section. They were seriously engaged with the music and the color changing LED lights, but the vibe I felt from one of the faces in the crowd, didn't come across as friendly. A woman ogled me longer than a minute. Her gaze was so intense when we locked eyes, my skin froze. A chill traveled down my spine, waiting for her to blink. Her menacing face didn't budge as she wanted my attention. My gaze didn't break either, returning her message was received.

I turned away and pretended the song currently playing was my jam to get out of the staring competition. Then it dawned on me. I recognized her silhouette, her long face, and her dark eyes. She was the mysterious woman in the photograph Mash and I never discussed. The bitch I wondered about from time to time. Mostly when I was pouting over something silly.

'How do I play this,' I thought. *'Should I lock eyes with her again, then roll them when she stares back, or do something clever to make her jealous?'* Jealousy won.

Winding my hips on the side of the stage, I eye-fucked Mash. His face turned pink and red, and his interaction with the crowd took a pause as he bit his lip on the side. His smoldering features turned serious as he signaled to some guy behind him, pressed a button on his equipment, then stepped forward towards me.

He placed his hands around my waist, and stopped them from winding. "I see Naughty Nadia came here tonight. You wanna quick one backstage?" he proposed. I moaned in his ear and smirked at the girl in the crowd studying us from below. She squinted her eyes as I showcased my effect on the man she obviously came to see. But he was with me.

If she didn't know me before, she knew me now, but I still knew nothing about her. Something told me I was about to learn more than I wanted to, but that lesson would have to wait, as I was too entranced with the man who put a ring on my finger. Naughty Nadia was at the party, and she wanted pleasure, even if it was against the dirty wall of a dressing room.

I placed my bag around the knob before Mash locked the door behind us. Forcefully, I unbuttoned his pants, and pulled the zipper down. He was ready without any participation on my part. I stroked his spear in my hands as his face pressed against mine, then we fervidly locked in a sloppy kiss. I could feel the speed of his heart increase with my hands wrapped around his love muscle, beating like a marching band. He fingered my orifice. "I knew you wanted me twenty minutes ago," he said, gliding my drip around the apex of my inner thighs.

I quickly squatted and licked a circle around his rim. He sighed of gratification, so I licked him twice more, then placed his head in my mouth for one quick suck.

"Ha-ah-ih," he respired, as his hands hovered above my head.

I rose to face him. "You'll get more of that later tonight."

He rotated our stances and lifted my right leg, pressing my back against the door. I panted in heat, anxious to feel his girth separate my walls. A gentle tug on my thong bared my pulsing flesh for his cock to stand up in my pussy with ease. Above my head, he gurgled sounds of pleasure from the tightness of my warm embrace. As he grunted I whined, bracing myself for the lashing my pussy was about to receive.

I clenched my juices around him and moaned. "Ah."

He grunted, then thrusted strong and long. "You know how to make me come quick. Don't you girl?"

Rhythmically, I timed each push until I was lost in the zone of our souls being weaved together as he came inside of me, grunting and breathing heavily, holding me so tight I couldn't move.

"You good?" I asked, jittering from a cramp forming in my toe.

"Always." He slid out of me gently.

"You better get back out there." I exhaled, then wrapped a napkin from my bag around the lining of my thong. "I'll be out shortly."

"I wouldn't dare leave you back here alone." He frowned, securing the zipper on his jeans.

Quickly, I made myself presentable, and we headed back to the stage arm in arm. The audience cheered at his return under the flashing lights. Maximus reveled in it, holding up his hands with a proud grin on his lips. I cheered for him, too, but mostly for the private performance I'd just received.

For the remainder of his set I behaved. No dancing. No enticing. Plopped in a provided seat, playing the good supportive wife idly standing by, secretly scouring the crowd. Unlucky in finding the face of what I sensed to be a rising problem.

2

EX-GIRLFRIEND

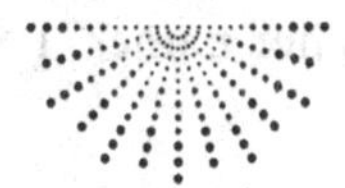

*W*hat truly happened the night in Cardiff, rose from the back of my mind from time to time. Mostly when I was PMSing and looking for a reason to bitch about something. Also, because there was no closure.

Ignorance is bliss to some. Count me out of that lineup. *If only I could let it go.* I started playing twenty questions in my head. *Why didn't he want to talk about this girl, and why was she making her presence known all of a sudden? — and on our second anniversary nonetheless.*

I kept quiet during the short ride to the hotel, purposely driving Mash insane. *He should have never let me know the silent treatment kills him.* He grew fidgety in the back seat, constantly knocking his knees with a balled fist, tapping his heels vigorously on the car floor. *He knew something was up.*

Either he saw her in the crowd, too, or my silence made him uncomfortable, and I was no holds barred once we reached our room. Calmly I asked, "Are you going to come out with it, or do you want me to belittle myself and ask the obvious?" He opened the balcony doors and lit the unfinished joint hiding in the crease of the window sill. If I could place a sure bet, he was carefully crafting his

9

response. And judging from the bullets of sweat forming above his eyebrows, I patiently waited for him to answer.

Orchestrated circle clouds of smoke left his lips until he killed the silence between us. "She is the girl in the photo that bastard Harv sent you."

"No shit Sherlock. Who is she?"

"An old acquaintance of nonimportance."

"So, you've said. What's her name?" I asked, not interested in the least.

"Nomi."

"What does she want?"

"How would I know? I haven't spoken to her."

"But you saw her."

"Apparently, we both did."

Mash tapped his gar against the brick and stepped back in the room. A breeze followed him inside as we briefly stared at each other, waiting for the other to blink.

"You know we never fully discussed what happened that night." My eyes pierced his.

"And you want to do that now? At 4 a.m.?" He scoffed.

"Why was she there?"

"Again, I haven't had any communication with her, and Nadia, the last thing I want to do is talk about an ex-girlfriend. We've had a great night, and it's our first time away together in months. Can we please table this for another time?" He begged.

"Fine. We'll finish this in the morning. Just know, I don't plan on asking you about this again. You need to come clean with me about whatever dirty little secret you have with this woman. Am I clear?"

"It's our anniversary and we're here for two more days." He sighed. "Why ruin it over nothing? Forget about her and enjoy everything I have planned for us. Okay?"

Fuming internally, I managed to utter, "Good night."

The presence of this Nomi heaux awakened the bitch in me Mash hadn't met yet. I clock watched during what was left of the night, thinking about the way she looked at me. Looked at him. Looked at us.

I practically lied on the edge of the bed, clinging onto the sheets to keep Mash's arm from covering me as he slept like a baby. Either he had nothing to hide, an innocent conscience, or the late set he worked had him spent. But he slept peaceful and sound, while I stared at him until the sun came up like a mad woman.

As anxious as I was to badger him in the morning, my mind imagined the worst. I needed a distraction and some space, and let him sleep in. My baggy eyes and restless body visited museums, tourist attractions, and a café on my list of sites and places to visit in the city. I declined all calls, then slowly made my way back to the hotel when I knew he'd be gone to his set.

The sleepless night eventually took its toll on me, while anger fueled my restlessness. My fickle mind chose not to stay in and sleep, but slip into a bit of mischief instead.

Posing as a regular patron, I lurked about in the darkness wearing cut off denim shorts, and a skinny black tank with a shirt tied around my waist, skimming the entry line for what's her face in the crowd. Behind chic glasses I bought earlier in the day, I hid my face and styled my hair in a bun, attempting to pass for a college girl.

Once I made it inside, I sat at the bar until the crowd overflowed the floor, then made my way upstairs to a table in the corner with a bird's-eye view of the dance floor. A white bolder hid my frame from the stage as I observed the room—anticipating I'd see Nomi's face in the crowd.

A text lit my phone from Mash.

Mash: *"At least tell me you are alright."*

I waited to respond as I watched him pick up his phone a few times in between songs looking for my reply.

Nadia: *"I'm fine. See you when you get in."*

The angst on his face humored me after he read my response. His shoulders raised and he smirked to himself. A thread of guilt swept over me for making him wonder of my whereabouts. *You better sweat,* I thought to myself, laughing internally at the change in his demeanor.

We wouldn't be at odds if I didn't feel he was withholding information. It was also possible I was all worked up over nothing, which wouldn't be the first time. I knew this man loved me. There wasn't any doubt in my mind he did, but whatever he wasn't telling me ate away my soul, and I felt justified in torturing him until he filled me in.

My poor clueless husband was now grooving with the beat, whereas before he looked bored on stage. I laughed out loud in front of a group of strangers standing near my table—Receptive of their stares as they weren't in on the joke. I continued to giggle at the sudden pep in Mash's step. *If only he knew I was watching him like a hawk a few feet away.*

* * *

MY PLOY of crowd surfing was a bust. There was no sign of Nomi after nearly two hours of searching through the horde, and Mash's set was coming to an end. I rushed to the exit hiding behind the people standing near the rail, wiggling between them when my gut spoke to me. *Don't leave just yet.*

I listened.

In an obscure spot across the street, I made myself comfortable leaning against an old foreign car whose name I couldn't pronounce. Watching the crowd of people come and go, I examined the faces under the buttery colored light above the club's entrance. Still, no sign of her.

A few feet away a pack of drunk clubbers hopping into the last cab freed an open space on the street. I eased over to the shadow where they stood, and caught a glimpse of the side entrance in the alley. Bingo. There she was with two females in her company, standing where Mash was due to come out.

I didn't smoke but I could have used a cigarette once I spotted her. The temperature of my blood rose to boiling, and my hands grew clammy with sweat. My chest was pounding so forcefully, I could hear it inside my head and swore I saw it thumped my tank top above my heartbeat. I took deep breaths stomping the pavement towards her, questioning if confronting her was the right thing to do. *Is listening to what she has to say going to bring me peace? And how will I know if she's telling me the truth? Fuck this, I'm ending this shit tonight, and letting my presence be known.*

I took my hair down and covered the top half of my body with the shirt tied around my waist, and blended in with the fans. Five minutes later the side door opened, and Mash walked out addressing his admirers, signing posters, and posing for photographs.

As he posed with a couple, one of Nomi's friends intruded, and pointed in her direction. They shared a look before she walked over to him, and my chest dropped into my stomach.

I stepped in closer and zeroed in on their conversation catching the tail end of it. "Leave me the fuck alone." Mash berated her in front of everyone. The crowd grew loud with gasps and chaos, and Nomi stood on her toes in his face.

"Don't be like that baby." Her lustful eyes looked into his as she dragged her whorish nails across his shirt.

I wormed through the horde and eased into their proximity, alerted by the madness growing from the bystanders. They pulled out their phones and began recording the commotion as Mash unleashed on the two of them.

"You and your friends need to stay the fuck away from me!"

I tugged on his shirt, and turned to the couple waiting for their photo op. "Did you need me to retake your photo?" Mash's eyes widened. "Baby, these lovely people are still waiting for their picture with you," I said with raised brows and a soft smile.

He returned my smile and posed with the couple, then took a

few more shots with patrons before taking my hand and hurrying me into the limousine. I didn't look at him.

"What were you...?" he asked.

I put my hand up to silence him. "We're almost at the hotel."

His hands trembled during the ride. I reached over and placed mine on top of his. He removed my hand, and placed his arm around my shoulder. The heat from his chest provided me with warmth from the breeze seeping in through the cracked windows. I listened it to race with the beat of my own, hoping our exchange would lead to resolve.

Inside our suite, we stood at opposite ends, waiting for the other to speak. "I'll go first," I said, studying the twitching of his lips as he gazed at me with narrowed eyes.

"Where did you come from?" he interrupted.

"What the hell is going on?"

"You first," he demanded, pacing the floor and running his hands through his hair and down his face mid yawn.

I took a few deep breaths and calmly answered him. "I couldn't sleep so I spent the day roaming the city."

"All day?" His voice heightened as he questioned me.

"Yes, all day."

"Nadia, we have security guards for a reason. You can't just wander off in a strange city you know nothing about alone. And when I call you, answer your phone for fucks sake."

I leered at him. "I made it back in one piece."

Mash stood before me and gripped my shoulders with his fingers. "Listen to me. Don't ever leave without telling me where you're going while we're traveling. Do you understand?"

"Yeah, I hear you."

"It was reckless and selfish. Anything could have happened to you. I could have been hurt. Or needed you..."

"I said okay. I heard you. I'm sorry. Wait. Why am I apologizing?" I removed myself from his clutch.

"Where did you come from tonight? You said you were here."

"And then I was where you apparently needed me."

"I did need you." His blistering tone simmered. "I do need you."

I escaped his hovering, followed by his shadow against the wall on my heels. I stopped short and turned to him. "People were recording you lashing out at those girls. It's probably all over the gossip channels by now."

He grabbed my hand. "Thank you."

"You're welcome."

His lips curved on one side. "So, you were spying on me?"

I scoffed and sat in the lounge chair in the corner. Removing my flats, I looked up at him and shook my head. "I wasn't spying on you. But I did see what I needed to see."

"Which was?"

"How you and your ex would act with one another if I wasn't around. I got my answer. Now, tell me. What does she want? And talk now or I walk."

"Enough of the leaving me bit. Nomi is not a nice person, and I'm being respectful of women with my choice of words."

"She's a bitch. I can see that first hand. But why is she showing up all of sudden? Getting in your face? Looking at you how I look you?" I pursed my lips.

Mash sighed then removed his shirt, baring his chest to entice me. *It was working, but I held my composure.* He lied back on the bed. "I told you I had friends when we met, and Nomi was one of the few I could call to come over and keep me company. We had some wild times, but that was then."

"Was she your girlfriend?"

"A friend. And the night in question something happened, but not what you think before you jump to any conclusions."

"Are you kidding me right now?" I threw my shoe at him.

He caught it with one hand. "I didn't sleep with her. Calm down."

"Sure you didn't!"

"When I made it back to my hotel room, she and the friend she was with tonight were in my room— naked. I told them to leave, some awful things were said, and I lost my temper and threw them out in the hallway. Nomi caused a scene and threatened she would tell the tabloids I assaulted them. I panicked, not knowing what other tricks she had up her sleeve. A hidden camera in my room perhaps. Who knows? So, I packed my bag and checked out. That picture is of me checking out."

"In that picture she was in your face?"

"She was high. Begging to have the room because the hotel was booked. I took care of the charges, but put the room in her name. I went to another hotel."

"You were in Cardiff for days. Three to be exact. How do I know you didn't have any other interactions with her? How do I know you really put two naked women out of your room? Most men dream about banging two women, and you dismiss a threesome like it's nothing?" I rolled my bracelet off and threw it at him.

Mash chuckled. "Been there, done that. Nadia, I'm not new to this scene. Alcohol, cocaine, ex, orgies— it's all history now."

"Cocaine and orgies? Iyiyi."

"That is what they wanted tonight. Access to drugs and a hookup."

Hearing two women approached my husband to fuck and fly didn't sit well with me. I knew his lifestyle could get wild, but seeing it in real time disturbed my soul.

"Can we go to bed now?" he asked.

"Suddenly, I'm not tired." I mumbled.

"Do I hear a challenge?" Mash fled to invade my personal space.

"You wish." I pushed him aside. "And let me be clear. I'm not inviting another woman into our bed."

"Neither am I. I'm not sharing you with anyone." He picked me up and threw me on the bed.

Stealing kisses from my neck while I squirmed beneath him, I interrupted his attempt to kill the conversation with affection.

"How do you think they got in your room?" I asked, placing my hand between his lips and my cheeks.

"Davie is the logical answer. Though he denies the allegation."

"You had plenty of chances to tell me all of this." I lied still under him.

"Babe, nothing happened."

"Proof of your innocence would be great. I mean, I can't blame Nomi for wanting another night with you, but I'm having a hard time shaking the jealousy I feel. I think I want to leave in the morning."

"No." He stated, calm yet stern.

"Excuse me?" I shoved him from on top of me.

"You will accompany me tomorrow night. You will be seated close to the stage, and we will leave together. End of discussion?"

I didn't respond. I felt his demand in my bones, and knew that was the end of our argument. His explanation had given me a headache, and my chest tightened lying next to him during our heated moment.

I exhaled deeply, then headed for the shower. Once again on my heels, Mash followed me. Fully undressed, erect, and aware I wanted no part of him.

Pressed against my back, his cock jutted, begging for my attention. My weakness for his touch normally caused me to cave, giving into the satisfaction of him fucking my brains out, figuratively and literally. The mental elevation and higher vibration we journeyed together when physically connected made it hard for me to say no, but I fought off the urge. I avoided looking into his eyes, kept my back to him, and cleansed my body swiftly, wanting him in the worst way.

Refusing myself pleasure and residing in my anger, led me to revisit the few heated disagreements we had. Discord that led to some of our best raging sex moments. This felt like it could be one of those times, but I was determined not to fold. Determined not to look into his eyes, which I could do for hours, and resist the temptation of the one-eyed monster I craved rigging my oil slick. *Not this time.*

Playing hard to get excited him even more. *Always up for a challenge this one.* He pressed deeper into me, as if I didn't recognize the firmness of his penis moments before. His hands glided across my shoulders, massaging them with kneading thrusts as the soap from his fingers lathered my back.

I allowed him continue to work my body because it felt too good to stop. Allowing his fingers to slowly slide everywhere they pleased until I was covered from head to toe with white bubbles.

I stood still, facing forward towards the shower head, getting lost in the sensation of his manipulation. He then reached for the cloth in my hand, and scrubbed my back in mini circles, touching all of the sensitive spots that required his touch and attention.

Growing weaker by the minute, my eyes rolled back and my posture wilted, in his hands and by his hands. I replayed his story in my head, believing his words to be true, but still wanting some form of proof. I needed it. My pride required it to not feel dumb for taking him at his word.

Now pulsating between my drenched cheeks, he rinsed my body, using his pillowy lips to delicately suck the water beads from the back of my shoulders. I imagined him already inside of me, locked and loaded with a full hard on, as he toyed with my body from behind— rinsing away the lather on my breasts with palms of water, while teasing my neck with his tongue.

I exhaled in heat, like melted putty in his hands. His fingers skid south of my navel with an intended purpose to flick my golden spot. I tensed knowing if I let him touch me there, I was his to devour, so I turned around to face him, and kissed his cheek. "Thank you." I grinned, then exited the shower.

Quickly I dressed for bed in one of his t-shirts and pajama pants, jumped beneath the covers, and pretended to be asleep when he toweled off in the room.

"You left me hanging in there, but don't worry. I took care of it myself. I haven't had to charm the snake in a long time, but I still love you. Good night." He climbed in behind me and laid his arm over my waist.

I cuffed my chest tightly and squeezed my lips, trapping laughter in my throat. Quietly, I swallowed each chuckle, feeling the burn from his eyes down my back.

Mash never liked when we went to bed angry. Over the course of our short marriage, I was the only one with the bad habit of doing so. No matter the fight, disagreement, or misunderstanding, his arms always ended up wrapped around me, and this time was no different.

By morning, he rose as if all had been forgiven. I declined his invitation to see the city, and barely spoke a word to him all day. By nightfall, I did as he ordered and accompanied him to the club, adored him for the cameras during his set, and waited for him in the car while he mingled with his fans.

While Mash was signing autographs and posing for pictures, I spotted Nomi staring at me through the lightly tinted window. A deep sigh parted my lips and a heavy load pressed inside of my chest at the sight of her. I have never cared for confrontation in my life, but her presence disrupted my peace.

I slipped out of the car on the opposite side of Mash, irrational, tense, angry, and annoyed. As I approached the nuisance, my thoughts were unclear and led by anger.

Pointing my finger in her face I warned her. "I will say this once. Let this be the last time I see you hanging around my husband. If you see his name on a flyer, or hear he is in the same city as you, alter your plans."

"Aren't you cute. Keeping my spot warm while Maxi has a tantrum. Don't get too comfortable." Nomi smirked and shared a laugh with her friend.

I giggled. "He said you were a bitch. He really does know you well. The stunt you pulled in Cardiff has earned you a spot on my hit, I mean shit list, so if I were you, I'd tread lightly."

"Enjoy him while you can. It won't last. I'll never be out of his system." She turned to her friend again, cosigning her every word.

"This ring says you've been out of his system for a while now, and from the way he screams my name, I'd say enjoy those memories you're holding on to. I hope you enjoy the rest of your desperate night, and stop embarrassing yourself. Has been."

With a fake smile laced upon my lips, I waved good-bye to Nomi and her friend, bumping into Mash who I assumed was rushing over to my rescue. His knuckles formed in one hand as the fingers on his other hand tapped the side of my stomach softly. "You okay?"

I nodded.

"What were you doing?" he asked.

"I put an end to this ridiculousness." I gritted through my teeth, and placed my palm on his chest.

"Are we good?" He kissed my forehead.

"In time we will be. Can we agree, I deserve some time and space to process all of this, and sort it out for myself?"

"How much space and how much time?" He slammed the car door shut.

"However long it takes." I squeezed his hand, searching for support in his eyes.

3

GIN & COCONUT WATER

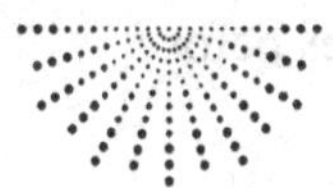

The will power I possess to scoot away from the hardness pressed below my cheeks in the middle of the night, and early in the morning should be awarded. After days, sometimes weeks of my doing so, it begins to wear thin for the both of us as its punishment— For him and me.

Though I suffered from the lack of his touch, and placed a border between us with a body pillow that magically ends up on the floor by morning, I held true to will of no intimacy. Using no sex as punishment was not my finest hour, especially when it carried on past a week, and I had grown comfortable in the petty game of tit for tat, forgetting what we were at odds about.

I woke one morning and inched over to his side of the bed. It was cold and empty. I searched for Maximus throughout the house with no luck, realizing I had become the villain, and couldn't quite process how I allowed the tables to be turned on me— Despite my infantile behavior of making breakfast for one, ordering takeout for one, and stocking the cabinets with the foods I liked. If that wasn't enough, the drawn out silent treatment, and never responding to his *'I love you'* texts, had sent him over the edge. Some days I texted a response, and was certain he saw the moving dots on his phone, but

I couldn't bring myself to press the send button. And that morning I felt the repercussions of my silly actions. I had gone too far.

Everybody plays the fool at some point, but when it's your turn it's sucks pure ass, and I was in a terrible, frustrating state to say the least. Ironically, the hurt I felt during that time decided to move on without my permission and tell me we were over it, waking me to an empty bed and an empty house, waiting to receive the '*I love you*' text I ignored so many times before.

* * *

WORK WAS slow which gave me time to reflect on my anger issues, dedication to vengeance, and inner she-devil I oddly found satisfaction in. I had watched Mash sulk all week, but it was my turn that morning.

The noise of the city served as the perfect distraction, yet my thoughts wouldn't allow me to write. Every word flowing from my pen expressed feelings of sorrow, regret, and the absence of love, and the delete button left me with a blank computer screen staring back at me. Still no text from Mash.

After studying the pixels on the white page for minutes unknown, finally I composed a script regarding a fictional account of my true feelings of the turmoil at home. My insecurities about the beautiful— I hated to admit that— ex-girlfriend lurking about. I tapped into deep, buried anger, jealousy, and personal struggles I'd locked away from previous heartbreaks. One in particular.

Thoughts I never shared with anyone but the page as the words began pouring out of me. My keys tapped nonstop, potentially creating my first masterpiece until my focus was disturbed by the bells chiming above the front entrance, and a velvety male voice asking, "Is anyone here?"

I stuck my head out from my office. "Hello. I'll be right with you." Quickly, I threw my blazer around my shoulders and stepped into the lobby area. "Sorry about that."

"The lights were on so I let myself in." He smiled.

The image went along with the voice, and did not disappoint. I hadn't seen a chocolate man this handsome since I left the states, and I wondered where he had been hiding. I eyed him from head to toe, then laughed internally at my thoughts. *Of course, a handsome stranger would turn up when I'm on the outs with the hubs.*

Hardly servicing any customers, I had to pull myself together. I erased the grin on my lips and cleared my throat. "Pardon me, how can I help you today?"

"I'm looking for Nadia Melton, or Nadia Sharper." My last name lingered on his lips.

"It's Sharper, now. And you are?" I scowled.

"You're Mash's wife?"

"Yes, I am. How do you know my husband?"

"We run in some of the same circles. He's quality on the tune scene. Huge following from what I hear. Mint guy." He grabbed the new growth of chin hair on his beard.

Carefully I crafted my response after watching his fingers smooth the roughness of his beard. "Please forgive me for not following. I am still learning the use of some words over here. I'm not sure what mint guy means."

"Sorry, it means he's cool." The gentleman chuckled.

"Then yes, you do know him. What can I help you with today? Are you interested in purchasing a home?"

"I am, but I'm also here to discuss another matter with you. You submitted a project to my production company, and I wanted to meet with you to see if you were open to a few changes, and possibly working together."

"Seriously? Which title?" The excitement in voice escaped me.

"The short story entitled 'Run'."

"Ha! What a way to end my day," I said, placing the closed sign on the door.

"You know I never forget a face. I saw you in Cannes a few years ago. You and Mash were on my yacht."

"I remember being on a fancy boat, but I didn't know anyone there. To be honest all I remember was smiling and shaking hands with people, and mispronouncing names."

"It is a pretty busy event, and select crowd. I understand."

"Forgive me if I seem out of sorts, but I'm in shock to hear about my work. After a while I gave up it was well received."

"I found it fresh. You should be proud of your submission. Let's say we schedule a few meetings to discuss your script, the changes I have in mind and so forth, then later arrange a meeting with my fiancé about seeing what homes are on the market."

"Most definitely. Excuse me while I fetch my planner."

His eyes followed me as I left the lobby, so I contained my shimmy dance until I was fully inside my office. I saved my masterpiece of emotions on my laptop, then returned to the lobby with my calendar cued to schedule the appointment.

"I didn't catch your name." I asked a second time.

"Yohan Stallworth, but my friends call me Yogi." He reached for my hand.

"Nice to formally meet you, Mr. Stallworth." I reached forward to shake his.

"Please, call me Yogi."

A tingling sensation traveled from the back of my hand, up to my shoulders, then into my chest. His handshake was firm and short, but I could feel the strength residing in them. I sighed to collect my wild thoughts and hid the frustration rising from the impossible openings he held in his calendar. My schedule was wide open, landing three meetings within the next two weeks— One day to meet with his soon to be Mrs., and two days to discuss the direction of my script.

An embarrassing rumbling sound from my stomach imposed during our chat.

"I apologize. I haven't eaten anything all day." I hid my face behind my hands.

"I could use a bite to eat myself. I'm free for the next few hours.

What do you say we have our first meeting right now, and continue this conversation over a working dinner? My treat."

"I'll grab my purse."

Mr. Stallworth reeked of wealth. His cologne smelled as if it were made specially for him, and his skin shined like chocolate silk. I assumed he spent time at spas getting facials, exfoliated, and groomed by staffers tending to his every need.

The suit he wore was custom made and tailored to fit his physique precisely. The more I glanced over him I felt intimidated, and I didn't understand why. Mash introduced me to a life of money, but Yogi's presence felt like a different kind of money— like longer money, and I was positive he had more of it.

I cheesed like an idiot during the walk to his car. I couldn't shake off my level of excitement, knowing one of my works had finally caught the eye of someone who could help me reach the level I aspired to achieve. Two years ago, I was aboard this man's yacht, and now a guest in his luxury Mercedes, being chauffeured to a working lunch. *What were the odds?*

The driver parked curbside, directly in front of a Jamaican restaurant a few blocks away from my office. It had been a while since I incurred the spicy flavor of jerk chicken cooked correctly with rice and peas, and the moment we walked inside, I nearly *foodgasmed.*

I ogled at the edible meals on customer's plates as we were seated, immediately ordering an appetizer. "Plantains and coco bread please." My voice dragged as I pled. The waitress smirked and giggled to herself while placing a fork and knife rolled into green paper in front of me.

"*Ya* familiar wit' Jamaican cuisine." Mr. Stallworth surprised me, speaking with an island accent.

"I know my way around a Caribbean menu." I nodded. "I didn't pick up on an accent earlier."

"It comes out when I get around my people. When I'm conducting business, I code switch so I'm easily understood."

"I see." My eyes stretched, noticing his eyes were more hazel than whiskey brown.

"You look uncomfortable. Did I say something wrong?"

"Not at all. It's just when I first came here I wasn't treated so well by a Yardie. It wasn't anything serious, but he caused me a great deal of headaches."

"Wha ya know 'bout a Yardie? Was he a romantic interest?"

"He wanted to be, but didn't handle rejection well. He had a horrible ego, and was really disrespectful to me."

"All man not the same. Don't judge us as one. I can't speak on his behalf, but he should have known better. Jah teaches us to respect thy woman."

"Thank you." A curve rose from the corner of my mouth.

"Look. You're smiling again. All is right with the world."

While waiting for the apps to arrive and place our order, Yohan showcased a mixture of professional Mr. Stallworth, and Yardie Yogi. We touched on my story, topics pertaining to black culture in the states, the U.K., and in his native homeland of Jamaica. I took notes of our conversation for a documentary idea I had in mind about the history of our people I hadn't executed as of yet.

The waitress returned with the coco bread and I stuffed my face while ordering jerk chicken, rice and peas, mac and cheese, with a side of curry chicken for later. Yohan copied my order, except he chose a side of yams and curry goat with a gin and coconut water.

He explained the changes he wanted to make to my piece, and the direction he pictured the short film could expand. Time got the best of us as we ate our dinner, talking for nearly two hours, as refills of water settled the spicy tongue I missed dearly.

"It's getting late Mrs. Sharper. I must be on my way to another appointment."

I checked my messages. "Yes, I need to be on my way as well. I enjoyed our meeting, and I look forward to working with you."

"Welcome aboard." We shook hands once more.

The chauffeur parked next to my car. Yogi, in gentlemanlike

fashion, opened and closed my door. The driver waited for me to leave the lot, then pulled out behind me as I merged onto the highway. *Still no text from Mash.*

Having not heard from my better half, I dialed Khai, and shrieked lightly into her ear. She put me on pause, then connected us on a conference call.

I screamed louder. "Guess who has a short film in the works!" I gasped for air.

"It's about time someone gave you a shot!" Khai exclaimed.

"Who are you going to be working with? And is this a paid opportunity?" Shannon asked.

"I don't know the money details yet. I have to find an agent, a manager, a publicist. Just look up Yohan Stallworth."

"I'm pulling him up right now. Let's-see-what-we-are- working-with." Shannon sang. "Damn!"

"Damn is right." Taylor cosigned.

"He is a seasoned brother, but never mind him. How are you and Mash going to celebrate tonight?" Khai asked.

I scoffed, debating if it was time to discuss the drama with the dreaded ex. Again.

"I'm a little salty with him at the moment, but this would serve as reason enough to make peace."

"Why are you being mean to my friend?" Khai sassed.

"Remember the infamous picture?"

"Yeah." They answered simultaneously, then the line fell silent.

"Turns out some shit did go down that weekend."

"Oh hell nah!" Shannon exploded. "Did he cheat on you?"

"You two always go to the extremes and come up with the worst possible scenarios." Khai fussed.

"He says he didn't, but you know how my mind works." I sighed.

"And why don't you believe him?" Khai chastised me.

"Because the story is cockamamie. His former manager came up with some hair brain scheme, which led to some sort of disturbance, forcing him to check into another hotel, and it all sounds a bit too much. I told y'all how I felt about the ridiculous staged photo business mess. That girl has been a huge thorn in my side. She has threatened and stalked him. I had to step to her."

"You did what?!" Shannon bellowed.

"It's a long story. Since I put her in her place, we haven't seen her since. But still, her presence lurks and it bothers the hell outta me."

"Don't allow that heifer to drive a wedge between you two. If **your husband** says nothing happened, you should believe him. You don't want him to think you don't trust him." Khai advised.

"Well I... um... do trust him. But it feels foolish not to question the matter since he shares a past with this girl. Ya know?"

"Nadia, go home. Tell your husband your good news, and apologize, to him." Khai instructed.

"Why am I apologizing?"

"Because I know you've been giving that poor man the silent treatment?" Khai added.

The phone call went silent until the giggles from Shannon and Taylor created an uproar.

"You and your grudges." Shannon cackled.

"Whatever. It's times like this I wish you all were close by. Y'all should come see me for a few days. What if I buy the tickets?"

"I would love to getaway, but I've been put on bed rest until I deliver this baby." Taylor groaned.

"Is everything good?"

"Hypertension is getting the best of me, and my feet are swollen all the time. I have to keep them elevated, but everything is fine."

"I'll be there when he or she arrives. What about you Khai? Can you come hang with your best friend for a few days?"

"If you are buying. I am flying."

"No need to ask me. I'm not turning down a free trip." Shannon added. "Now go home and slurp on *dat* hummus, so you can swipe his card and buy these tickets."

4

RED LIGHT SPECIAL

usic from the studio blasted all the way to the garage when I arrived home. I was sure Mash saw me arrive on the cameras, but the music never paused, and he didn't come upstairs to welcome me home. *He was definitely pissed with me.*

I showered, then hung out in my bedroom texting back and forth with Khai while researching flights for the upcoming visit. The positive energy of my day compelled me to do as she instructed. I shrunk my pride and prepped an apology to end the feud.

Being isolated on what had become my side of the house during our fight, should never have happened. I felt silly for allowing the distance to grow between us, and even worse my own friends weren't on my side, subtly telling me to grow the fuck up.

My chest felt the pain of our discord the closer I approached the loud session in progress, deafening me once I entered the studio. The room was tinted blue from the borealis lights glowing from the corners, and Mash's face tightened at the sight of me. I rarely made an appearance in his workspace, which I assumed the reason he looked staggered as I stepped towards his station.

The music continued to thump as my heartbeat increased, and

29

the hairs on my arms raised. I looked around the room, stepping over cords taped to the floor, and noticed Prano sitting on the sofa. He waved and I waved back, still watching my step, careful not to trip.

Mash was seated behind a slew of mixing boards and complex looking equipment. He stood and reached for my hand, and guided me into his station. His finger pressed against his puckered lips instructing me to be quiet, then he surprised me with an elongated kiss. The instrumental began to fade and the song stopped playing over the speakers. In my ear he mumbled, "Is everything okay?"

"Yeah," I answered, wanting another kiss.

I stood on my tipped-toes and took one more toke of his missed sweetness. He looked into my eyes and smiled as I leered in his face. He knew I wanted him, but did I deserve him was the question.

"This is wrapping up shortly. Okay?" He assured me, slipping his hands down to my ass. "You've avoided me for a long time. Is everything okay?"

"I don't want to fight anymore."

He grinned. "It's about time."

"And sorry for interrupting your work. I didn't know you were recording. I couldn't wait any longer to say I'm sorry."

The voice singing when I entered the room spoke through the speakers. "Did you forget I was in here?"

"Essence come out and meet my wife." Mash signaled towards the recording booth.

"Finally, I get to meet the woman who stole my party buddy. It's nice to finally meet you," she said, stroking the back of my hand.

"Nice to meet you, too." I inched my hand away from her grip.

"You are stunning. Prettier than Maxi led on."

"Thank you." I raised a brow, staring at her hair, unsure of which color to focus on.

"We hug around here. Bring it in. You're family now."

"Essence, keep it PG." Mash's voice deepened as he turned on the lights.

Essence smelled of fruity hair spray and day old marijuana. Her blonde, pink and lavender locks looked better than they did in the blue light— eye catching to the point I couldn't look away. She stood about my height, maybe an inch shorter, and her hug was lasting a little too long for my taste.

"Mash, play what we just created for these fresh ears." Essence continued to hold on to me.

"Oh no, I never get involved in his business. I was just poking my head in." I eased from her grip.

Mash turned the room back to blue with the push of a button. "I want you to hear it."

"I'm parched." Essence grabbed her throat. "Can I pour you a glass while I'm serving myself?"

"I drink red."

She returned with my wine, and I joined her on the couch, listening to the new song they recorded. The tune was catchy and upbeat, forcing me to hum along with the melody. When it ended, I stood and congratulated them on creating a hit, then excused myself.

"Don't leave me in here drinking alone with these two." Essence grabbed my hand.

"I suppose I can sit for a few minutes more."

Across the room sat Prano scrolling on his phone. He and I hadn't seen one another in weeks, so we chatted for a bit until Essence interrupted our conversation. "Mash, I think Nadia should go in the booth and do some adlibs." I stood again to leave and she grabbed my hand. "I heard you harmonizing with the melody. Go in there and give it some spice."

I declined and pried my hand from hers. Mash called me over towards the boards. "You wanna try?" His eyes gazed into mine.

"No." I aimed for the door.

His hand covered mine on the knob. "Let me hear what she's talking about, and we'll be done in here. Come on. For me?"

After failing to escape, I found myself slightly tipsy in front of a microphone, surrounded by darkness, with Mash's voice instructing me to hum the melody as I had before. Making a complete ass of myself, I repeated the words of Essence's melody singing through the headphones, missing the beat, and fumbling the words.

"Told you I was no good at this." I huffed.

"You're fine. When I point to you, give me what you got. And try to have fun with it." Mash winked at me.

As I waited for my cue, I goofed around in the booth, blurting whatever came to mind in the microphone— having fun with it. A few takes later I had done what was asked of me, and rejoined Essence and Prano back in the lounge area as Mash worked his magic.

Moments later, the music echoed over our conversation, and my equalized voice harmonized behind the lead vocals. I was mortified at the sound of my voice. Essence and Mash, on the other hand, screamed they loved it.

I sat on the sofa in horror. My face red from humiliation. My heart pounding at the sound of my voice. I placed my head between my knees, and rocked front to back, when the sensation of fingers stroked my ankles, slowly working their way upward.

"We could do so many things together. You, me, and Maxi," Essence whispered.

I jumped up and the music stopped.

"Essence, we are wrapped for tonight!" Mash shouted across the room.

"Are you sure we got it?" she asked.

"Oh, I'm sure." He chided. "Prano, thanks for driving Essence out tonight. Be safe on the road." He nudged her towards the front door.

"Nice meeting you." I waved goodbye, walking alongside Mash.

He secured the house and together we watched Prano's car disappear on the camera. I walked towards the hallway and waited for him. Briefly our eyes met when he turned the corner.

"She was a pit," I said.

"A what?"

"A pit. It's what we call aggressive women in the states. Like a Pitbull."

"Trust me, she's worse."

I scoffed. "Interesting choice of people you hang around."

"I've known her for years, and I don't hang. I work."

"You're right. Poor choice of words on my part."

"Come back downstairs. I want you to hear something." He reached for my hand then escorted me back into his sanctuary.

I hovered over him as he zoned out, squinting his eyes and curling his mouth as he tweaked buttons and pressed switches. The track we recorded played in the background, and near the song's end he pulled me close. "Check this out." He grinned on the side of his mouth, then kissed me.

'Deejay Mash you are turning me on.'

Shame overwhelmed me as I laid my hands against his chest. His grin grew into a huge smile as heat rushed to my face. I swallowed the gulp of air trapped in my throat. "Tell me that's temporary?" My eyes blinked more than a fading light bull.

"No. This is now my official tagline."

"I was playing around when I said that. You told me to have fun with it. Delete it, please?"

"I'm taking this to get mastered tomorrow. Now let me hear you say it to my face," he commanded.

I rose from the sofa. "I will do no such thing. Delete it."

"Say it." He pinched my ass.

I wiggled from his grip. "Un-uh."

Mash pulled me into his lap and sucked on my neck. Like ice on a furnace, I instantly melted from the touch of his hand at my waist, and his lips nibbling through the cotton of my tee arousing my breasts. "You've deprived me long enough," he muttered. "Tonight, I'm going in." He carried me to the narrow entrance of his work station.

"Says who?" I giggled.

"Says you. I can feel your pussy throbbing for me." He grazed his teeth on my ear lobe, laughing devilishly while placing his fingers between my legs.

I squealed as he grabbed my lower back and placed his hardness against my pelvis. "I missed you," he said, lifting my tee above my head.

"I missed you, too." I sighed into his mouth.

"Let's see how much." He thrusted two fingers down my yoga pants and parted my folds. "Ah, this won't take long. But I promise I'll owe you one."

"I keep score, remember?"

Foreplay was unnecessary. I had been wet for him the moment I inhaled his scent and he kissed me. My body needed his touch, and my warm embrace pulsed with excitement knowing he was about to be inside of me. "Yes!" I moaned as he roughly lowered my pants to my knees, bent my legs in the air, and plunged inside. Vigorous and steady.

I returned the favor and grazed his ears with my teeth gently, accepting the pain of the slight tear in my open wound. Mash clutched the back of my upper thighs from below, guiding me back and forth on his dick. I held on as I cursed, belted, shouted, and blasphemed. "Oh God!" I bellowed as my walls gyrated from the joy of his girth.

A day was too long to not feel his stiff, perfect timber. I was overdue for this thrashing, but as he said, it wouldn't take him long. His strokes grew wickedly intense, and his hands shifted to my cheeks, bounding me closer and harder on him. With growling obscenities flowing from his mouth and a trembling stance, his cock ballooned and exploded. "I'll never put you on punishment again," I whispered, caressing the arched muscles on his shoulders.

He found the strength to carry me back to the sofa while my pussy gyrated around his dick. Short breaths and weakened from his release, he held me up until I finished raining on him, then threw me on the sofa as he fell to his knees. "Get up here." I reached for him.

"There's no room."

"I won't have you on the floor."

He rose to his feet, and lifted me from the couch.

"I was under the impression that workout tired us both." I wrapped my arms around his neck.

He laid me on the sofa in the living room. "This one can hold us both. Let's sleep here tonight." He slurred, climbing behind me.

5

HIT ME BABY ONE MORE TIME

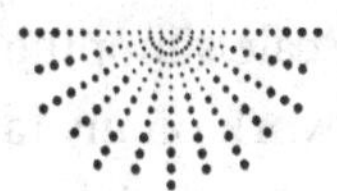

The sound of birds chirping outside woke me which meant I was late for work. Covered with the blanket resting on the arm of the chair, and snug in Mash's arms, I wriggled from his hold, quickly showered, blended the mix for the pecan waffles he loved, then ran off to meet my only appointment for the day.

It was off to a perfect start. My physical needs were met, my mind relaxed, Yohan extended an invite to Paris for one of his events, and a huge commission was in process as I ended my no sale streak.

I returned to the office to process the paperwork in high spirits, counting the money from the sale before it was complete— a bad habit I needed to break, but couldn't resist picturing the zeros dropping into my bank account nonetheless.

With the rest of my day clear, I proactively researched locations to present to The Stallworths. I scrambled from one task to the other, too busy to notice how fast the morning hours passed by. Noon was behind me when the chimes on the door jingled.

I stepped out of my office. "What are you doing here?"

Mash stood in the doorway. "I didn't know I needed an appointment?"

"Never." I smiled.

"I had some time to kill while my files are being mastered. Thought I'd treat my wife to lunch."

I beamed along the drive towards the West End of London, praying we would stay on good terms as we passed below the haloing angels. Our makeup sessions after a spat made discourse between us worthwhile sometimes, but seeing happy couples walk hand in hand along the upscale shopping district gave me a sense of guilt, and introspection to work on my faults.

Attentive as always, Maximus picked a quaint café on my list of dining options I'd recently mentioned. We ordered two appetizers and an entrée to share, taking turns dipping the chips in the queso.

"You seem lively today. What gives?" he asked.

"So much. I don't know where to begin."

"Lucrative morning?"

"Yes." I screeched lowly. "I made a sale."

"Congratulations. I was hoping you were glowing because of me." He smirked.

"You, and the commission I'm going to make once the I's are dotted and the T's are crossed."

"It's nice to see you smiling again."

"Love, I owe you an apology. I was done being mad at you a week ago. I don't know what I was waiting on to come to you, but I kind of felt like you weren't fighting for me. And somehow I became the villain in all of this."

"I texted *I love you* every day, and you never replied."

"I know. I was wrong for not responding."

The light in his eyes dimmed. "That's not good enough for me."

The rise of my cheeks sunk, and the weight of the previous weeks returned to my shoulders, shifting them south along with my mood.

His dark, sad eyes looked into mine. "Last night was great, but we need to have a serious talk."

The seriousness in his voice shook me. "I thought we were okay since…"

"What? We fucked and connected like a husband and his wife are supposed to? Nadia, we won't survive if you continue to behave the way you do."

I leaned forward. "How dare you bring me to a public place to chastise me."

"People have problems and shit happens, but it's how you handle them that determines whether you sink or swim. And you cut me off as if I mean nothing to you."

"So, I deserve whatever this is because I gave you the silent treatment?" I scoffed.

"You know I hate it, yet you do it instead of communicating. I know I love you more than you love me, but I would never act as if you don't exist. Life is short, and I need for you to do better."

"You do realize we were, or as it seems, are still at odds because of something you did. Right?"

"What exactly did I do? Not tell you about something to prevent you from being angry. Nothing happened. I need to know if you believe me or not?"

"I…"

I couldn't answer him honestly. Even when I hated him, I loved him, but in that moment I was cross— Heavily pissed by our conversation, horrified of his tone, and on the verge of going down the dark road of petty pride to hurt his feelings because he was hurting mine.

"Yes or no?" He badgered me.

"Yes, I believe you." I lied.

"Good." He adjusted his seat. "This is for you." He slid his phone across the table unlocked. "I paid handsomely to give this to you." He pointed to a picture of the hotel receipt from the weekend in Cardiff. "Slide right." He motioned his fingers as if I needed instruction of what to do when a video prompt appeared on the screen. "Press play."

"I don't want to see this." I sighed.

"I think you do. You needed proof, so press play."

"I said I believe you."

"And I thank you. Now watch."

The demanding tone of his voice led me to press the triangle. Footage of the night in question began playing— Mash walking into his room alone, and moments later shoving Nomi and her friend out into the hallway. Naked.

I stopped the recording.

"Carry on," he said, smug and righteous.

The video continued and showed him leaving the room shortly after the girls were thrown out, then cut to him in the lobby at the front desk, checking out like he said.

His eyes pierced mine. "I wanted you to see this so there would never be any doubt about my word."

"I said I believed you. What more do you want from me?"

"Your absolute trust. You say you trust me, but I don't think you do. I don't think you trust anyone."

"Trust is hard for me."

"Come off it, love. Trust is hard for everyone. Haven't I done enough to prove you can trust me?"

"But I do— trust you."

"Not completely. You doubt my word. You've left me, ignored me, and cut me off until you're ready to shuffle me back in. Frankly, I..."

"I'm over this." I cut him short and stormed away from the table.

In the midst of my theatrics, I left my jacket on the back of my chair, shuddering at the corner telling me to look left in bold print at my feet. As the breeze chilled my body, I was reminded of my earlier thoughts to think before I react. If I had I wouldn't have been cold, leaning against the front of the car for warmth in the parking garage.

The heat I felt internally as I fumed at the unexpected direction of the conversation, and the jabs delivered by Mash's words bleeding my heart did not provide me with warmth. Nor did the lingering curiosity of how he was going to finish his last sentence. *What was he going to say? Frankly? Frankly, he was what?*

Minutes later he walked up behind me with Styrofoam trays in one hand, and my jacket in the other. He placed my jacket around my shoulders. "Let's go," he said authoritatively. I shrugged away from him and slid near the passenger door, waiting for the lock to click.

Painfully I sat in his car swallowing every obscenity known to man. My eyes more than rolled. They cut him like sharp blades attached to a windmill. Before I knew it, a tear deceived me and fell. I wiped it away swiftly, then focused on the blurry cars passing by, and the hazy faces inside of them until I shut my eyes, praying for a moment of clarity.

The car twisted and turned then finally stopped. I opened my eyes, expecting to be parked outside of my office. To my surprise, we were parked in front of an old, brown abandoned building.

Mash wiped away the disobedient tear trickling down my cheek, embraced my hand, and frowned. He'd seen me cry before—at movies, or from stumping a toe on the dresser, but never like this.

"Where are we?" I exhaled long and deep.

He squeezed my thigh. "I know you're pissed at me, but I want to show you something."

"I'd rather you finish your sentence from earlier."

He let go of my leg and huffed. A few seconds went by and he leaned over and unfastened my seat belt. "Let's go inside."

"I don't want to. This place looks run down."

"It has character. You'll see."

I followed him inside the rusty building, wondering where we were, why we were there, and praying it wasn't an investment he was about to talk me into after the café cliffhanger.

"Smitty!" he shouted.

"Who is Smitty?"

"An old friend. This is where I trained as a boxer. Hello! Smitty! You here bud!" he yelled.

"I don't think anyone is here," I said under my breath.

"Someone is always here."

Dragging footsteps from afar caught our attention near a faded, painted hall at the back of the dingy room.

"Who's shouting in here as if they own the place?" A withered voice grumbled from a distance.

"Come see!" Mash shouted.

The frail silhouette made its appearance from the back hallway limping slightly to one side, swimming his arms through the air to help make way for him.

"I see a woman, but I heard a man's voice," he said.

"Over here old man." Mash chuckled.

"My eyes deceive me. Maximus?"

"In the flesh."

"Look at you with hair on your face. The boy is now a man." He patted Mash's back. "What brings you by son?"

Mash shook his hand and tapped his shoulder. "Nice to see you too, Smitty."

"Are you lost? I thought you gave this up?"

"Actually, I wanted to know if you could string us up?"

"Us? You and who?"

Mash looked at me with puppy eyes and kissed the back of my hand. "Where are my manners? Smitty, this is my wife, Nadia. Nadia, this is my dear old friend, Smitty."

"Nice to meet you sir." I waved, keeping my hands to myself. "But I have no idea why he asked you to string us up."

"Can you do it Smitty?" Mash insisted.

"I sure can. Get in there."

He led me to a set of steps and escorted me through the ropes. I took off my jacket and my heels, then gave Smitty my hands. He taped them, then tightened the strings on a pair of used black gloves. I wiggled my fingers inside the cushion, laughing internally at the seriousness on Mash's face punching a speed ball.

Smitty exited the ring. "She's ready for you!" he shouted at Mash, heavily engaged with the flow of punching the air ball near the wall. A few hard and final strokes later, Smitty praised him. "You still got it boy." Then he covered him with head gear, and a body pad.

Without taping his hands underneath, Smitty laced Mash's gloves, then held the ring rope open for him to climb inside. Mash moved around on the mat, showing off his footwork while punching the air.

I stood with my hands on my hips. "Why are we doing this?"

"Your job is to hit me." He danced and jabbed.

"I don't want to hit you."

"I think you do."

He was correct in his assumption as I had weeks of aggression to release. I posed to one side and lightly drove my arm to his chest. "Humph. There, I did it." I stepped backwards to my corner.

"Hit me like you mean it," he ordered. "Use all your might."

I swung again, this time using all of my strength while moving my feet. The punch landed on his arm and he grinned. "Much better. Hit me again." I took a big swing with my right hand, and another with my left, landing blows to the side of the padding, and surprising him with a jab on the tip of his chin. Mash looked at me as if he were proud. "Again."

I begged to stop, but Mash continued to encourage me to let loose, and hit him with conviction. "Use your legs and pivot when you throw." He instructed.

"How long do I have to do this?"

"Until you've got all of your aggression out. I know you want to kick my ass, so kick it. We aren't going home until you've got it all out of your system."

"You should have led with that."

I squared up and went in for the kill this time, imagining he was Nomi, Dylan, and even Isla. I swung wildly and paused, then punched him wherever the improvised blows chose to land. He blocked most of my shots, but I could feel the tension and anger in every punch I landed lift the load from my shoulders.

"Kick his ass darling!" Smitty cheered from the sideline once I found my groove, cornering him against the ropes.

"Why does your ex-girlfriend think she still has a shot!" I yelled, landing a punch to the padding on his headgear.

"She is delusional." His muffled voice added. "Don't believe anything she says. Please."

"Does a part of you still love her?"

"Absobloodynot!"

Mash still had the moves, blocking and dodging, dancing and ducking the majority of what I threw at him. The jabs and body shots I landed were mostly achieved out of pity, with one or two wild shots stunning him on the sly.

When I nearly passed out from exhaustion, Smitty rang the bell. "I've been at this long enough to know when it's quittin' time. Good job darling."

Mash held me in his arms so I wouldn't fall. "Are we good?" he whispered, taking off his headgear.

My face rested against the pad and I hummed. "Um uh."

"Still mad at me?"

"A little bit, but not really."

He laughed at my response. "No more fighting. Just love making from here on out," he said, kissing my forehead while I continued to catch my breath.

Smitty cleared his throat. "You two are always welcome to come here and work out your lover's quarrel. That was quite entertaining." He chuckled.

Slowly I crept to the car. The smell of my abandoned lunch hit my nose when the door opened, and I attempted to eat what I could before making it back to the office, only to shut my eyes before the fork reached my mouth.

The engine of the car turned off and I woke up.

"Carry me inside." I whined.

Mash leaned over and kissed my neck. "I'd rather take you with me."

"I need to put away my files and look over my schedule. I should be heading home in about twenty minutes."

"I can wait on you to finish. We can leave your car here overnight." He insisted.

"I'll be fine. Just don't take all night coming home. I have something to discuss with you."

"Tell me now."

"It's good news. I wanna tell you later so you can give me what you owe me. Remember?"

He kissed my cheek. "You do keep score."

I dragged my body inside the office and locked the door behind me. Sluggishly, I reviewed the properties for Yohan and his fiancé, then stood alert as the chimes on the door clunked and whistled.

"I could have sworn I locked the door." I mumbled to myself, then grabbed the baseball bat behind my office door.

Slowly I crept out of my office.

"I'm here to settle my debt." Mash kissed my open mouth.

The bat fell to the floor as Mash pushed me back inside the office. He nibbled on my neck, closed the door behind us, and pressed my back against it. I was previously aroused from our battle in the ring, but the sensation of his hands roughly rummaging under my blouse made me want him even more.

Fast paced motions burgeoned my breathing. My jacket was thrown across the room...My blouse slipped over my head, and tossed to the floor.

Mash slowed down the pace for a hot second, stood back, and surveyed me. "This looks new." His eyes gazed on my breasts so hard the clasp between my mounds loosened.

"I bought it in..."

"Shhh." He centered his finger across my lips, then pressed on the bottom to part them. "Anytime you speak you will be punished." He warned, sliding his finger inside my mouth.

I pulled on it and moaned. "Okay." I tested the waters, curious of the punishment.

"Un un uh. You spoke. Turn around." He commanded.

I turned towards the door with my hands pressed against the glass. He roughed me up by the waist and slid his fingers down my slot, slowly unzipping my skirt. While strumming his fingers over my bikini, he dropped my skirt to the floor. *Whapp!* His hand slapped my cheek.

The shock of it startled me. "Oh." I jumped and turned to look at him.

He stepped forward. "Who told you to turn around?"

"I..."

He twisted my face forward towards the glass. *Whapp!*

My pussy throbbed and my nipples hurt as they hardened against the glass on my door. A kiss where his spanking landed increased the heat bursting inside of me. I shivered, then melted like butter as a soft lick, and open-mouthed kiss wet my ass. Succulent licks mixed with a combination of sucking on my ass cheeks until his tongue popped had me climbing the walls, but in this case, climbing against the door.

"Now you may turn around." He decreed.

I obeyed and faced him, wired, full of flames, and in heat like a desert.

"On your knees." He directed the top of my head below his belt.

I knelt down like a submissive schoolgirl, and reached for it.

He smacked my hands away. "Do as your told."

I sat on my hind legs and waited for instruction, watching him meticulously unbuckle his pants, waiting for his smooth dick to spring forward.

A wicked laugh released above me. I looked up at him, catching a grin on his lips.

"You love this cock, don't you?" He rolled the tip around my lips.

I nodded yes, then remembered I would be punished if I spoke. "I do." I sighed.

He waved his finger side to side. "A simple nod would have sufficed." He lowered his briefs and his cock burst free, tapping against my forehead.

Mildly clutching a fist full of my hair, he rubbed the tip of his weaponry around my lips again. I gripped it with my mouth, fast and tight, making him call out to the heavens. While he sent worship past the ceiling, I turned my head sideways, and placed him in between the bottom of my tongue and the floor of my mouth. His cries of delight assured me I had him positioned in the right spot. He hummed sounds of maximum pleasure while I tortured his soul with my jaws and tongue swirling around him. A trick I learned to weaken his knees.

My willingness to make him feel like a man, and put forth extra effort to explore him sexually fucked him up physically and mentally. In doing so I nearly choked, pulled back, and went forth again after a minor break to catch my breath and recuperate.

"You like that, huh?" I smiled.

He grabbed a lock of my hair and stuck his dick down my throat. "I didn't give you the order to speak."

I gagged and he jolted near eruption from the way my wet mouth glazed his volcano. He lifted me from the floor, and placed me on the edge of my desk. My legs spread apart and he slid inside.

I lamented and leaned back, holding on to the cliff of my desk taking the fast and rough stabs, losing my grasp. My slippery palms grabbed the lamp, but it fell from my hands. The stapler dropped beside it— The desk slid closer to the file cabinet, gnashing across the floor.

"Your debt is paid." I muttered below strained breaths, earning the punishment of a hair tug.

"Someone likes getting into trouble." He groused, pulling my hair tighter.

"Ah yes!" I respired, groaning at the second tug.

"You-are-asking-for-it."

He stopped mid-stroke, turned my back to him, and lifted one of my knees on the desk. His wet tongue lashed against my orifice and I shuddered. My nails screeched against the wooden surface as I hollered of delirium when I felt him charge back inside of my warmth, slow and steady. As soon as I became comfortable where his cock resided in my pit, he plunged deeper with full force, and held it sturdy seconds at a time, repeating the offense until he felt sweat form down the line of my back.

My knee burned against the wood, but I endured the pain. Forgetting about the discomfort once Mash gripped my shoulder blades from behind, and drew moons inside my pussy. I pictured how his ass looked winding me in a circular motion, then clenched my canal tighter.

He screamed of ecstasy. "Ahh! Goddamn girl!"

Sweat nor air could seep through the tight hold he had on my body as he filled my cup.

"Now my debt has been paid in full." He declared.

"You forgot about the interest. You'll never catch up." I teased.

He whispered out of breath. "What am I going to do with you?" Soft kisses traced across the back of my shoulders as he caressed my hips.

"Love me." I reached back and played with his hair.

"I will forever."

6

WOMAN TO WOMAN

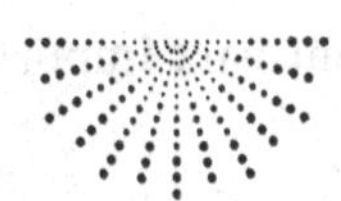

The hour was late when Mash arrived home. I was stretched out on the sofa when the sound of the garage lifting woke me.

"Nad!" He called.

"In here!"

He waltzed and jiggled the drive in his hand. "Got it mastered." He grinned before leaning down to kiss my lips.

A slight gush of wind blew my way when he plopped down next to me on the sofa. Mash placed his hand on my thigh. "Sorry I made you cry today."

I looked at him unsure how to respond.

"But why did you walk out one me?" He wrapped his arm around my shoulder.

"What were you going to say after, "Frankly"?"

He took a long pause and scowled at me. "What did you think I was going to say?"

"Don't do that." I shook my head. "Answer my question."

Mash lifted his hands and pushed back. "I didn't come home to fight with you."

"Then don't."

49

"What did you think I was going to say? You walked out on me for Christ's sake."

"Answer my question first." I folded my arms.

"I was going to say frankly, I deserve better and I want you to do better. And you have to control your erratic emotions. Take a pause. For me…Please?"

I huffed. "I will make the effort, and what I thought you were going to say in that moment isn't important. I'd rather tell you my good news."

"You refuse to play fair, but I'm listening."

"Do you remember the yacht we went on in Cannes?"

"Yeah, it belonged to a film guy named Han. Why?"

"Yes, Yohan Stallworth. He came to see me yesterday. He wants to bring one of my scripts to life."

"I see." His eyebrows raised.

"I was expecting you to be a tad happier for me. You know this could possibly be my big break."

"I'm excited for you, it's just Han has a slight reputation, and the film industry is shady as fuck. Shadier than my industry."

"What kind of reputation? Like ripping off people's work, or not paying artists?"

"Nothing of the sort. It's been said to never leave your girl around him."

"Really? I didn't get that vibe with him. He was a complete gentleman. Talked about his fiancé quite a lot, and they might give me the potential sale on their next home."

"Trust me. He is not going to get married. Don't be naïve, okay?"

"I won't. One more thing. This morning he invited me to this writer's symposium and premiere event. Khai and Shannon are coming to visit in a few weeks, so I was thinking they could attend it with me since you have a show that weekend."

"So that's his play." Mash scoffed.

"This is a huge opportunity for me. I could really use your support." I stroked his shoulder.

"And you have it. If this goes well you can stop pretending you love selling real estate, and invest in some of your other talents. Like opening a restaurant."

"Are you still on that?" I pulled away.

"You have no idea what you are sitting on. No one cooks like you over here. And you won't be in the kitchen always. Just until the place takes off running. We could make a killing. I'm talking early retirement. Just think about it."

"Let's see where this opportunity takes me first."

We agreed to table the discussion of my cooking and called it night. In the morning, I dressed the part for my wealthy clients— Expensive high heels, A-line dress from Saks, and designer tote hanging from my wrist.

Since Yohan looked, smelled, and breathed money, I felt the need to keep up in his presence, and that of his fiancé whom I researched before going to bed. Olive Lapois, five-eleven top model, slim with curves hard to miss, perfect topaz skin, and highly desired.

Beautiful women have never intimidated me. I always held my own because I knew internally another's woman beauty didn't dim mine— that is until Olive walked into my office. One look at her, and I knew my working relationship was safe with Mr. Stallworth.

I couldn't compete with how well put together she was from head to toe. Tall and poised, the pictures of her I found online didn't do her justice. She maintained her model figure post her runway career, and her bronzed skin glowed as if she just walked out of an esthetician's office with a fresh facial. She was absolutely stunning, and I couldn't help but stare at how polished she looked without wearing any makeup.

Being in her presence was the first time I ever felt as though my light dimmed, and I couldn't comprehend my sudden loss of confidence. My voice changed, and I stammered in my words until Yogi took over the conversation.

"Mrs. Sharper, meet the soon to be Mrs. Stallworth, Olive."

"Forgive me for staring. You are more gorgeous in person," I stuttered.

"Thank you. How sweet. I look forward to seeing what you've found for us today," she said, pursing her lips.

"I have three properties I think you'll be pleased with. Mr. Stallworth gave me a list of your preferences, so hopefully you'll fall in love with one of them."

"Yes. We'll see."

"Mervin, my driver will take us to the addresses if you don't mind." Yogi added.

"Perfect."

I watched how the couple interacted while we were driven to the first property, fixated on the fact Olive didn't compliment me in return. *Did she think I wasn't beautiful?* I wondered.

I sat quietly, pretending to look over paperwork, wondering why a sudden stammer took over my speech, and hated myself for appearing weak and subpar. I didn't like feeling inferior to her, and regretted not driving my own car where I could scream at myself in private.

The more she whispered to Yohan, the deeper my gut prepared me for a letdown. I kept my cool knowing beforehand I wouldn't be selling a house today, but carried on with the sales pitches I prepared.

Constantly smiling, and answering all of your majesty's questions, her distant stare proved my hunch to be true. Olive heavily critiqued the final house before we stepped inside. Yohan, on the other hand, never weighed in, or commented his opinion. Instead, he insisted we end the disastrous hours of house hunting to grab lunch, and discuss the hits and misses.

I wasn't looking forward to sitting down with Ms. Snooty Pants, but I remained hopeful a meal, and possibly a midday cocktail would adjust her attitude for the better. Sadly, I was wrong the pampered princess would be anything but herself. Not only was she cold towards me, she was also cold and rude to the wait staff, sending her plate back to the kitchen twice, and speaking to the poor fellow in a condescending, obnoxious tone.

Once Yohan settled the bill, and he and Olive led the way to the car, I pretended I left my phone and returned to the table. Our waiter and busboy were changing the linen cloth and wiping the seats as I interrupted. "Sorry about my friend. She behaves uncouth when she skips too many meals." The waiter snickered at my joke, casing our surroundings. I placed a healthy tip on top of the one Yogi left for him in his hand, then joined The Stallworths to wrap up the afternoon.

I jotted down Olive's significant change of home requests and must haves, and promised I would find her the home of her dreams without any intention of doing so. Once she was out of my sight I sighed of relief, thankful my Grams and mother raised me better.

My foot was heavy getting home. The smell of marijuana led me to the man cave, where I found Mash hiding behind a cloud of smoke. I envied how relaxed he was, looking at me with smoldering red eyes, and a grin of not giving a fuck, bounded by orchestrated O's blown from his mouth.

I placed my feet in his lap, removed the joint from his fingers, and took one good toke of whatever special blend he was enjoying. I held in the hit for as long as I could, then choked out of inexperience.

"Rough day," Mash asked, taking the joint from my hand.

I coughed for nearly a minute, then lied back and ran my toes up and down his chest. He knew what I wanted him to do and gripped my feet, settling me down with intense strokes against my instep. His hands soothed me as he traced my vein lines with his thumb, later forcing me to giggle when his lips kissed the bottom of my feet.

"I gather you didn't make a sale." He inhaled.

I rolled my eyes and lied my head back on the armrest. "I doubt I will with these two."

"You are dealing with the high-class crowd now babes."

"I actually feel kind of bad for Yohan. Olive is drop dead gorgeous, but cold as ice."

"Most wealthy people are." His voice rasped as he inhaled again.

"Do you know what my commission would have been if they'd bought any of the homes I showed them today?"

He exhaled a cloud away from me. "I assume huge. Do you need another hit to calm you down? You are acting as if we are broke."

"I know we're okay, but what we have is from all of your accomplishments. I want to know what it is like to make a lot of money on my own. I've borrowed and lived off of my mother for years. I'm waiting for the moment I can send her a big check and say thank you."

"So, let's write her a check." He sat up.

"With money I've earned." I kissed his lips.

"Why does it matter where it comes from? She is my mother now as well. Is everything okay back home?" He offered me another toke.

"She's fine. It's just an image I've had in my head for a long time." I swatted at his hand, then stared at the colored lights above my head.

"Have it your way, but the offer still stands. Maybe you'll get a big check with this writing project, or from the sale of this house."

My eyes shifted from the ceiling to him. "What do you mean this house?"

Mash smudged the blunt into the tray on the edge of the table. "I was thinking we should sell. Build a new house from the ground up. We can look for land when you come back from your trip."

"I'm game."

"And do me a favor. Don't be intimidated by Olive. Yohan is a pretty big deal, so of course she thinks she is, too."

"She is gorgeous."

"She is, but so are you. The woman I saw dancing to my set had all the confidence in the world. And she is still the most stunning woman to me. Always be that woman."

I wanted to cry, but the buzz I had going led me to laugh instead.

"Yes sir." I saluted him.

"I'm serious." His eyes gazed into mine.

"Okay. Hearing you say such sweet words, and rubbing my tired feet might get you some afternoon delight." I winked.

"Is this putting you in the mood?" His hands drew circles from my ankles to my calves.

I rubbed my feet back and forth against his gray sweats, and signaled for him to come closer. "Make me feel like that woman you just described." I lured him in.

Always up for the task, he didn't hesitate to strip me naked, and I stood above him exposed. "Turn on your recording equipment."

He smiled at my request and went over to the boards. "What do you have in mind?"

The room turned red, the equipment whirred and buzzed, and I stepped into the recording booth. Low toned and seductive, I whispered into the microphone. "Come here."

He eased through the narrow entrance. "What has gotten into you?"

I freed his cock standing tall for me. "Nothing yet."

His hand grabbed my face, the other gripped me firmly around my waist. His tongue coiled around mine sweet and gentle at first, then within a breath owned my mouth as his dick twitched against my thighs. He was ready to enter my warmth. I was ready to welcome him inside.

"You will not toy with me and make me wait for you tonight." Impatiently I sighed heavy breaths.

He sat on the barstool, lifting me high enough to get a quick taste. I moaned and grabbed a hold of the narrow walls and low ceiling, holding my balance with strained arms. Maximus placed his lips perfectly against my portal, robbing me of my honey like a bee in the spring.

Incapable of controlling my moans, I bellowed out. "Don't stop!" Holding his crown, I hummed and called him several names. "Maximus. Mash. Mr. Shaper. My Love. I'm ready." I begged to be breached.

With my hips in his hands, he sat me on his tip. I inhaled his cologne and weed stench, then exhaled upon his entry, gasping from the soreness of his cut. Back and forth I rocked as he lunged upwards in my throbbing walls, grunting and hissing while I wound my pussy, gripping him tightly and drizzling on his stem.

"Mmm babe. You feel so good inside me." I throwed my slit so hard I felt him in my stomach and flinched.

"I can tell. You're wet as fuck," he said, squeezing my ass and spreading my cheeks east and west.

"Ah, guide it how you want it," I whispered.

He grunted. "I love it when you come home wanting to get dicked down."

My hair stuck to my face from the steam we produced inside the claustrophobic booth. The sweat from Mash's chest made it easy for me to glide up and down against him. I sped up my rhythm, giving him the ride of his life, enduring the pain in exchange for pleasure.

My pacing and efforts excited Maximus so much in the suffocating hole we were in, he finagled me to the wall. "Allow me." He placed my right leg over his shoulder, then pinned me in a vertical split with him excruciatingly close and tight inside my walls. Grinding slow then hard, slow then hard again, I wailed, braying his name.

"Maximus."

"You know what that does to me." He grinded harder.

Fucking me deeper, and rougher, his hands cuffed my ass, leaving no space for me to escape, scraping my pussy from side to side, clasped together like the hook on a wire hanger.

I jeered and jolted until he joined me on my high, nearly squeezing the life out of me as he thunderously came.

"I fucking love you," he whispered.

With what wind I had left in me, I breathed down his neck. "I love you, too."

7

POWER TRIP

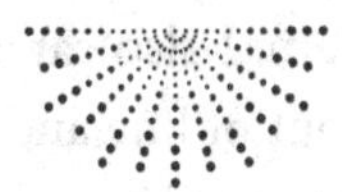

The next morning, I received a snippet of our recording. My cheeks beamed of fire at the visuals caught from the camera in the top right corner of the booth. "Damn I'm flexible." I giggled to myself.

The chimes on my office door sounded over the moans of love-making on my phone. I dropped it, frazzled a client heard me climaxing from my office. I shut down the message and poked my head out to the lobby.

"Am I interrupting something?" Yohan asked.

"No, not at all." I smirked, admiring his dapper attire. "I was just catching up on emails."

"Are you sure? You seem flushed."

"I'm fine. You caught me reading something hilarious from one of my girlfriends."

"One of the friends joining you in Paris, I presume?"

"Yes. One of them. She'd never forgive me if I blabbed. What brings you by?" I shuffled from behind the desk and sat with him in the lobby area. "I didn't think we were scheduled to meet again until after the symposium this weekend."

"I stopped by to have a word. If you have time?" He unbuttoned his jacket. "I saw what you did at the restaurant."

"I don't follow." My face wrinkled.

"I came back inside the restaurant to apologize, and leave a second tip to the waiter, but you beat me to it. Thank you, but you shouldn't have."

"I…"

"You don't need to explain. I also came here to apologize for my fiancé's behavior. She was out of line and behaved like a diva. If you were offended I totally understand."

"It's okay."

"Olive could learn a thing or two about being kind to people. What you did yesterday beguiled me. And if I know women, the way I think I do, I believe she is threatened of you."

"Me? Why? I'm sure you have plenty of mirrors in your house."

Yohan chuckled. "I do love that wit. I've spoken highly of you and your writing, and she doesn't like it when another woman has my attention."

"I really appreciate the compliment, but I— I, um, am lost for words at the moment. Actually, it was the other way around. I felt extremely nervous about impressing her, which is unlike me. I wasn't myself yesterday." I shook my head.

Yohan muttered. "Women and their competitive nature against one another."

I raised my eyebrows. "Excuse me?"

"Olive acted out of character. Now you are saying you weren't yourself. I don't know what brought on these different personalities yesterday, but to move forward, let's begin again. Olive really is a beautiful person. Inside and out. I think she may have sensed I have a slight attraction towards you, but I would never act on it. Our business is strictly professional."

"I'm glad to hear you won't cross any lines, and keep this new partnership professional. I plan to do the same. By the way, does Olive know I'm married?"

"She does now, but what does being married have to do with anything? People have affairs all the time."

"She wants a new agent, doesn't she?"

"You are quite instinctive. Olive definitely wants to hire another agent for our home, but she doesn't have any control over who I choose to do business with. I'd like to meet with you every day next week, except on Friday to get this project under way."

I exhaled and paused momentarily, shuffling through my emotions if it was worth pressing the issue of being fired as their realtor. *I shouldn't have counted those six figures before going into escrow.*

"How is four o'clock?"

"Four works for me." He grunted as he stood up and buttoned his jacket. "Also, I wanted to give you this for your time and trouble." He laid a white envelope on the counter.

My eyes focused on the bank label centered on the sealed packet. "I can't accept this. It wouldn't be right." I slid the envelope in front of him.

"You would have made a lucrative amount if we purchased a home from you, so please take it."

"I can't." I stepped behind the counter.

"You really are an impressive woman, Nadia. I don't take no for an answer. I'll see you and your friends on Saturday."

I locked the door behind him, and opened the envelope he left behind. A wad of crisp one hundred-dollar bills totaling to ten thousand dollars wasn't close to the commission, but the thought was impressionable. I placed the money inside the safe behind the picture on my office wall.

"Shit!" I exclaimed in a whisper. Thinking out loud, I paced my office talking to myself. "Mash would have a conniption if he knew Yohan gave me money. Is this what he meant about how people in the industry operate? Ugh. Keeping this a secret will end badly for me. I can't deposit this sum into our bank account, and if I send it to my mother, it would come up in a conversation somehow, and bite me in the ass."

Fully consumed by the distraction of the money, time quickly past, and I left for the airport later than I'd originally planned. I had come up empty with a solution by the time I heard, "Grandma Klump!" being shouted across the baggage claim area.

The arrival of Shannon and Khai satisfied my soul. We hugged and laughed on the terminal, made a spectacle bouncing like teenagers, and picked up where we left off as if time and space hadn't been between us.

I itched to blab about the ten stacks hiding in my office the moment we were secluded in the car. Khai could be trusted to keep the situation between us, but Shannon, the wild card, had a slip of the tongue from time to time.

They raved about the house. "Why are you putting this place on the market?" they both asked. I shrugged instead of going into detail, then showed them to their rooms, barely allowing them to settle in before forcing them out by the pool.

Shannon rolled two joints from Mash's stash I borrowed, and sparked a perfect doobie while we played catch up and pass.

"Did anyone else get the feeling Taylor was pissed we were coming over here without her?" Khai asked.

"Most definitely. She was short as hell with me when I called her last night," said Shannon.

"I'm worried about her," I added.

"This should be a happy time for her, but she has looked miserable since she's been on bed rest." Khai sighed.

Shannon nodded and exhaled a thick cloud. "She does seem miserable. I mean being held up in the house all day every day would drive anyone crazy, but like why aren't you happy? This is all you talked about before the wedding. Being a wife and having kids."

"Her hormones are all over the place." Khai mumbled.

We agreed with collective hums and head nods, passing the joint around until I giggled.

"So, what's going on with Isla? Is she still with my dreaded ex?" I watched the two of them share a look.

"Let me be the one to tell you, Isla thinks she is slick. She fakes like Evan is her end all be all, but I heard she was spotted out on a date with someone else. And guess what?" Shannon keeled over. "She's hummus shopping."

"Shut up!" I hollered.

"Yup. She still can't get over Mash checking for you, so now she is trying to match you white guy for white guy."

"I honestly don't know where we went wrong in our friendship. I mean Mash asked to meet me, not her. What was I supposed to do?"

"Exactly what you did. As a matter of fact, let me take some pics of this house to piss her off some more." Shannon cackled.

"Use the portrait filter." I smirked.

Mash snuck inside during one of our laugh fests. He walked out to the pool and gave us a simpering look, then grinned at us choking on his smoke.

Greeting me with a kiss he gloated. "Is everything alright out here?"

"Everything is perfect!" Khai shouted. "Why would you want to sell this house?"

Laughter flew from his mouth.

"She gets loud when she's high," I said.

He reached for the joint and pulled a short. "I can see that."

"Am I loud?" Khai looked at all of us.

Mash exhaled. "You can be as loud as you want. Consider yourself home while you're here."

"I was going to do that anyway." Shannon chuckled.

"And to answer your question, the wife and I are going to build a new home perfect for us. How have you ladies been doing? Seems like ages since I've seen you both."

"I'm doing fucking great over here in your land, chilling in your house, smoking on your shit." Shannon raised the joint with a hand salute. "Damn I wish you had a brother."

"It's always good to have you around Shannon." Mash snickered.

"Well, I'll let you get back to your girl time. Luv needed this visit. Babe, I'm going to bed. You ladies have a good night."

"I'll be in soon." I blew him a kiss.

Once the coast was clear, we continued our conversation, sharing secrets, and giggling like school girls.

"In the morning, we are going for a power walk before our flight." I mentioned.

"Oh shit. Something's afoot." Shannon put out the joint.

"Did you say afoot?" Khai and I gasped then laughed.

"I knew you were holding back." Shannon shook her finger at me.

"It's nothing, but it's something. We'll talk— In the morning."

"I'm too excited to go to sleep. Living like you rich folks for a few days." Shannon danced.

"I'm not rich. I'm blessed. And a little lucky. Let's turn in. We have a full day tomorrow."

I double checked the girls had everything they needed in their rooms, then joined my husband sound asleep in bed. I cuddled under him from behind.

"What took you so long?" he asked.

I squeezed him tightly, and nudged my face in his back until I needed air. "I came as fast as I could. Go back to sleep."

"How is everyone, really?"

"Fine. Go back to sleep." I adjusted my feet under his leg.

"You're happy." He smiled with his voice.

"I am."

"I'm glad they came." He gripped my hand.

"Me, too. Love you."

"Love you, too."

We woke in the morning, quietly sneaking a thorough session in before Mash's flight to Berlin. I saw him off before the girls and I drove to the school a few blocks away to walk around the track. Shannon burned with questions and guessed random, ridiculous situations until her imagination drew a blank along the short drive.

"What's going on besides you and Mash making the bed springs squeak?" Shannon teased.

My mouth dropped. "I beg your pardon?"

"I heard y'all this morning." She snickered. "I was about to knock on your door to ask you how to work your weird coffee machine, but I turned around when I heard you trying to moan all cute and shit. "Yes Papi. Unh, unh, ah. Give it to me. Good morning Mr. Sharper." She laughed out loud.

"Shannon!" I screamed.

My face glowed of shame as I threw air punches towards her, landing one on her arm by accident.

"Don't Shannon me," she said. "I'm proud of you girl. I thought you might've been a lousy lay. I was wrong. You got a little spunk in you."

"You thought I was boring in bed?"

"You know how you can act boujee sometimes. And boujee girls can't fuck. They are too busy acting cute."

I stopped walking.

"But you're the good boujee kind. A fun, lovable boujee bitch." Shannon smacked my ass.

"Um, Thanks?" I questioned with a scowled face and picked up the pace.

"Never mind her. Now tell us what you obviously didn't trust talking about at the house. You scared Mash got the house bugged or something?" Khai asked.

"You never know." Shannon and I high fived. "Okay, so here's what's up. The Yohan guy I'm working with gave me some deep compliments— and ten thousand dollars in cash yesterday for my time, since his fiancé basically fired me."

"Ten thousand dollars?" Khai frowned. "Please tell me you didn't keep it."

"It's in the safe at my office. He wouldn't take it back. I told him I couldn't accept it."

"And why didn't you tell Mash?"

"Because he didn't want me to work with him in the first place. Claims he has a reputation," I mumbled.

"What man doesn't have a reputation?" Shannon preached. "But for ten thousand dollars all I hear is Jay-Z in my head right now."

"Which song?"

"Have an affair, act like an adult for once." She sang.

"I remember that line. But it's only a song. Not for real life situations." Khai reminded us.

"Or is it?" Shannon raised a brow.

Khai and I rolled our eyes at Shannon.

"What are we going to do with this one?" I asked.

"My mama has been asking that question since I was five and the answer is nothing. Y'all are worrying about the wrong thing. It's a free stash of cash sitting around in your office. What are we going to do about that?"

I sighed. "I can't put it in the bank. I can't tell Mash about it. I'm screwed all around."

"I think you should tell him." Khai slowed down. "Let him be the one to give it back."

"But then he will forbid me working with Yohan. My one shot at success will be over."

"Let's see how this weekend goes. If your boss turns out to be a creep, tell Mash about the money when we get back."

"Iyiyi. I don't want Mash to be mad at me. We've been doing good since we settled the dispute over what's her face. Which reminds me, check out the video footage he gave me as proof."

We huddled on the track and watched the clip. After viewing it, Khai nagged. "Have you ever acknowledged I was right?" I ignored her and walked a little faster. She sped up and pulled the back of my shirt at the neck. "Now do you trust him?"

"Yes, I do."

"Finally. Trust is everything in a marriage, and you struck gold." She pinched my forearm.

"You know I hate playing the fool."

"Who doesn't? But we all do at some point. Hell, he's playing the fool right now. His wife has ten stacks hiding in her office— From another man."

I hated when she was right. "I see your point."

"Everybody plays the fool, sometimes." Shannon sang.

I checked the time. "We need to head back to the house ole wise one and off key one."

"Ha ha." Shannon laughed. "Don't worry. I have your back. I'll make sure you don't get into trouble this weekend."

"I don't need a chaperone."

"Hmm. We'll see."

NO NEW FRIENDS

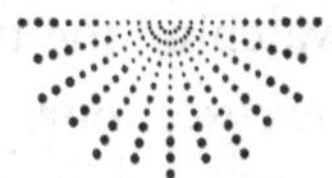

$\mathcal{M}$r. Hunt took care of me and the girls, thanks to my better half. Yohan reserved a spacious, furnished apartment on the top floor of a hotel for the three of us with a breathtaking view of the Eiffel Tower from the balcony.

We checked in, and wasted no time heading out into the city. The saying, *funny how time flies when you're having fun,* proved to be the case for us roaming about town, forced to rush back to change into our first looks of the evening for a kickoff mixer inside a ritzy white tent in the hotel gardens.

Yogi and I acknowledged each other with a nod as he and Olive were inseparable for most of the night. I laid low with the girls until they became star struck, then found myself a corner to people watch with a libation in my hand.

Shannon being Shannon, found her groove and gained us an invitation to a few after parties. Before heading off to the first gathering, Yogi made his way over to meet the girls, and offer his staff's services during our stay.

Shannon sized him up. "Which after party should we attend?"

He blushed at her blunt and bold stare game. "Definitely the one at the Grand. I'm headed there myself. I can give you girls a lift."

"Will Olive be joining you?" I asked.

"No chain tonight. Models and their beauty sleep. What are ya gonna do?" He shrugged.

"Then we'd love to join you." Shannon grabbed his arm.

The tension rose between Yohan and Shannon in the car, and continued at the after party as the only conversation the two of them were interested in was the one amongst themselves. Khai and I sat quietly at our table, watching the two of them ignore us. She and I shared a look and excused ourselves from their company. Neither acknowledged when we stood and strolled into the crowded room.

Filled to capacity with a better turnout than the previous mixer, the scene felt less pretentious, and the selection of music made me wonder what Mash was doing. I wondered if he was thinking of me in that exact moment? I smiled at the thought until I skimmed the dance floor, and noticed Shannon grinding on Yohan. Khai left me stag and accepted the hand of a stranger to join our wild friend, so I found myself at the champagne tower alone, observing everyone have a good time until Maximus called.

"How is it?" he asked.

I excused myself to the lobby. "It's going well so far. The rental we're staying in is a dream."

"Yohan has the means. He wouldn't skimp."

"There is something I need to tell you though." I slurred.

Maximus sighed. "And here it comes."

"Let me tell you first, jeez. Anyway, Olive fired me. Yohan felt bad about it, and gave me some cash for wasting my time."

"What!"

"I told him I couldn't accept it, but he insisted. It's in the safe at the office."

The silence killed me on the line. My phone nearly slipped from my hand as my palms turned greasy.

"Didn't I tell you he was shady?" His voice echoed on the line.

"You did, but..."

Mash cut me off. "He knows you don't need his money. He knows I'm not broke."

"Maybe, but I honestly think he gave it to me as a kind gesture. He said he knew I would have made a lot of money if I had sold them a house. Anyway, you should be the one to give it back to him — After my project is released."

Mash scoffed. "Yeah. Okay. And when will that be?"

"Three to four months depending on how smooth casting and filming goes."

"I can't make any promises."

"Don't ruin this for me."

"I only agreed to this catastrophe because you want it so badly."

"Babe, hold that thought."

My nature of minding other people's business hadn't vanished since leaving the states, and the fact that Yogi had a sly look on his face, and getting keys from the front desk caught my attention.

He slipped into the elevator.

Mash diverted my attention back to him. "Babe, what are you doing?"

I whispered as if Yohan could hear me. "Not minding my business. I just saw Yohan get room keys, and slide into the elevator, but he and his fiancée are supposed to be staying in the same hotel as us. Oh hell no."

Shannon sashayed over to the elevator. The doors opened, and Yohan stood inside grinning at her. I waited until the doors closed, then sprinted to catch the floor number it rose to.

"Luv? I told you he wasn't going to get married." Mash snickered. "Does Shannon know about Olive?"

"She does. At least you know he's not after me and can stop worrying." I sighed.

"Don't be naïve. I love you. I have to go. Keep me posted on Shannon's Shenanigans." He laughed.

I took the next ride up and found an empty floor. I walked the hall slowly, listening for Shannon's exuberant voice echoing through the walls. Crickets. I double-backed towards the elevator. Still crickets. Then suddenly the sound of thumps brushed against the wall of room 517. I eavesdropped outside of it, pressing my tired face covered in makeup against the door, and there I heard the voice I was looking for.

"Oh shit, Daddy. You are working with a monster. That skinny bitch *don't* know what to do with all this dick. Let me show you how we do it in the dirty south." Shannon roared.

Then silence.

Seconds later I heard. "Uman! What ya do ta me?" Yogi's raspy voice and native tongue surged through the door. "Ya sure ya not Jamaican gal the way ya throwin' dis pus."

"Uh, Uh, you a got-damn horse!" Shannon shrieked. "Yes baby. I feel it in my back you rough riding motherfucker!"

I slid away quietly…Humored, upset, and intrigued. Shannon behaved exactly as I imagined in the bedroom, but choosing to do so with my new boss infuriated me. I didn't know whether to be amused at what I heard, or pissed in the moment while parts of me wondered just what in the hell was she doing to him.

I held myself, then covered my ears on the elevator ride back down. I could still hear them going at it in my head with the music blasting at the party as I searched for Khai. She was off doing shots at the bar with a group of men. *What the hell is up with my friends?* I wondered. I knew Khai worked hard, took care of her family, and rarely got time to herself, but being surrounded by a horde of men getting shitfaced was out of character. What Shannon was doing, not so much.

I made myself comfortable near a fountain trickling water from its base close to the entrance of the hotel. Alone at the party. Alone with my thoughts. A tap on my shoulder woke me from my daze.

"Hey. I've been looking for you." Shannon grinned.

I unfolded my arms and scrunched my nose. "Really?"

"What's wrong with you?" She shoved my shoulder.

"Nothing. I'm just ready to leave. If you guys want to stay I can take a taxi."

"We came together and we're leaving together. Where's Khai?"

I pointed to the bar.

Yohan ordered the driver of his car to lift us back to the apartment. Shannon adjusted herself numerous times during the drive. Khai was too inebriated to notice, but read me well.

"What's wrong, Nadia? You look sad." She hugged me. "I'm so happy we're together again."

"I told Mash about the money."

"What did he say?" Shannon asked.

"He wasn't happy about it, but agreed to play along until my project is complete." I bit my nails and stared out of the window.

"I don't think he has ill intentions. He appears to really be interested your work." Shannon added.

"So, you don't think the compliments and the cash were inappropriate?" Khai scowled.

"Think of it as an incentive. Or a bonus." Shannon suggested.

"I'm normally right about these things. It's a way of opening the door to wanting something— eventually," said Khai.

"I seriously doubt it." Shannon bragged in a singing tone.

"Let's table this until the morning." I huffed. "I need to make sure Mash doesn't act out and ruin this for me. He knows how these rich people operate, and can fly off the handle at times."

By morning, I had come to terms that Shannon was simply being Shannon, and the anger I felt towards her shifted to Yohan the more I thought about it. His actions didn't align with his speeches, and his flirtation had thrown me for a loop. I didn't appreciate the head games, couldn't figure out his angle, and saw him as Mash painted him out to be now that he had fucked one of my best friends, with plans to marry a woman who fired me.

The perplexity of it all created a weird vibe at breakfast. The girls and I ordered room service, and sat quietly at the nook with secrets between us.

"Are you in a better mood this morning?" Khai asked me.

"Yeah. Mash and I talked more last night. Everything is cool."

"You can tell Mash he has nothing to worry about. I took care of your problem last night." Shannon boasted.

"How so?" Khai stopped eating her croissant.

"I slept with Yogi last night. Nadia is in the clear."

Khai dropped the piece of broken pastry in her mouth into her lap as Shannon continued.

"While y'all were downstairs, me and moneybags were upstairs and voila— Afterglow." She waved her hands around and twirled.

Khai turned to me. "Why don't you seem surprised?"

"Because I saw them last night."

"Is this why you're acting salty?" Shannon scowled.

"I'm not acting salty. I'm just praying it doesn't affect my work dynamic with him. He's the ticket to my personal success. I need this project to go well, so I can be known for what I'm good at. Not for the person I married."

"Well Nadia, you should be thanking me. I did you a favor. He was skipping when he left last night."

I placed my fork on my plate. "Did you two at least set rules, or boundaries? And what about Olive?"

"What about her?"

"And Manny?"

"Manny is at home, and I am over here. Anything else?"

"Nope."

"Good, now let me tell y'all how Yogi is a Bear."

Khai and I jumped up from the table. "Spare us the details please, Shannon."

"He blew my back out. I know he is a heaux 'cause brother man got the goods. I recommend every woman have sex with him. It's a share piece. You get a piece, and you get a piece." She joked.

Khai and I looked at each other and laughed.

"Promise you will be on your best behavior today. I'm sure his fiancée will be watching him closely." I asked her holding up praying hands.

"I know how to handle these situations, Nadia. He isn't my first rodeo."

"Ya don't say."

* * *

As special guests of Yohan, we entered the screening before the red-carpet experience. I took notice of how the panels on stage were arranged, and learned questions were given to selected audience members beforehand. *Crafty*.

Seeing the writers and producers in action aroused my fear, and made me doubtful I belonged. They were poised and composed in answering the questions prepared for them. I was nowhere near ready for such a spotlight. "That's going to be you up there one day," Khai whispered, squeezing my hand. I turned my head to hide the tears forming in my eyes, recomposing myself before the lights turned on.

The main event concluded, and the crowd gathered down the hall at the after party— it was boring compared to last night's events. We mingled with the cast and crew of the film, learning most of them were pretentious assholes once they turned off their camera charm, bragging about who they were, why they were famous. From time to time, I tuned out of the conversation and searched the room for anything interesting to keep me awake.

Shannon and Yohan appeared to be having a moment from across the room, which caught my eye until an arm wrapped around my shoulder. A gentleman had eased between myself and Khai, placing his hand as if it belonged...As if we were familiar.

I looked past him over at Khai, stone-faced and still as night. "What the fuck?" I mouthed. To my rescue, a waitress infiltrated the circle with hors d'oeuvres. I grabbed the tiny fare, and removed myself from his unwanted advance.

My stomach turned as I exited the room, finding myself on a bench outside the arrival station facing the busy street buzzing along. Mash's words struck a chord deep within me. *"The film industry is shady as fuck."* I hated he was right.

I was just getting my feet wet and already felt the pressure of imposter syndrome, harassment, and possible cash for favors. My skin wasn't thick, and my naivety didn't know how to deal with the vileness of this new world.

Sulking in front of strangers as the concrete pierced my skin through my dress, I stuffed my mouth with the quiche bite I took from the tray, gobbling it in public like I would in private.

The smell of rich bergamot travelled up my nose. "Can we talk?" Olive stood above me.

Please don't let this be about Shannon and Yogi.

I closed my mouth and nodded.

Of course, she would walk up on me while I was smacking like a pig, or a person with no home training.

She leaned over so her luxurious, flowing, long hair could fall to her side. "Firstly, I owe you an apology. I didn't feel comfortable around you, and wasted your time trying to find us a house. I should have met with you, and had a conversation before I told Yogi to find someone else. I'm sorry for the way I handled things."

"Thank you. I appreciate you sharing this with me. I was wondering why we didn't get on."

"Every woman knows their man. I wasn't sure if Han was dangling you in my face to get a reaction out of me. Men like him need attention. But I can clearly see you have no interest in him." She giggled.

"None. No offense." I held up my hands.

"I also saw what happened in there." Her eyes glared and eyebrows raised. "The hand on your shoulder? We women are often subjected to unwanted advances in this business. The behavior of the men in this setting is intolerable, but you handled it well."

"Do you know who he was?"

"No, but I'll see if I can get a name from Han."

Khai emerged with Shannon on her heels. "There you are. We've been looking for you all over the place."

I stared into Shannon's eyes. "Girls, I'd love for you to meet Olive, my boss's soon to be wife."

"Hi. I'm Khai."

"And I'm Shannon. Congratulations on your engagement."

Khai and I inhaled together. Our faces froze in suspense at Shannon's pleasantry. Olive smiled with curiosity, towering over the three of us.

"Thank you. Lovely to meet you both." She grabbed my hand. "Nadia, I'll be in touch. If I don't see you before we leave, have a safe trip back. Talk to you soon love."

"Thanks again for the kind words." I placed my other hand above hers.

Shannon waited for Olive to turn the corner. "Talk to you soon, love? What the hell just happened?" She sat on one side of me, and Khai the other. "Are you best friends with her now, love?" Her lips tightened.

I scoffed. "She was comforting me."

"For what? You know you can't be friends with her since I'm fucking her man."

"You'd know why if you weren't busy flirting with her man inside, and I doubt she wants to be friends with me. And what do you mean you're fucking her man? You slept with him once— so…"

Shannon grinned. "We'll see about that?"

Khai silenced her. "Does Olive know the man who got handsy? When you left, I heard someone refer to him as one of the producers."

"Figures. That means he has money, and thinks he can grope whoever he wants. You hear these stories all the time, but never thought it'll happen to me. You know?" I shook my head.

"Show him to me. I'll ask Yogi about him tonight." Shannon blurted.

I leered at Shannon. "Please don't screw this up for me. If Olive finds out about you and him she might tell him to scrap my project. Don't get caught up…"

Shannon cut me off. "I know what I'm doing. Let me enjoy myself before I'm on permanent lockdown. Now, allow me to handle my business."

I scrunched my face watching Shannon tip out for the night.

Khai whispered, "Wonder what lie your boss is going to tell your new friend to creep with your old friend?"

I sighed. "It's been a long day. Let's call it a night."

Under a starry, midnight blue sky and lights in our peripheral, Khai and I enjoyed trays of room service on the balcony. Over laughs, trading marriage stories, and tales of our days as roommates in college, I cut a deck of cards, and she dealt while reliving secrets we kept between ourselves. I laid down the first card and munched on fruit, waiting for Khai to play. Her eyes bulged and she blew from her mouth before throwing an ace to claim the book.

"Our *fivesome* became a foursome when you left, and now we're a threesome with Taylor on bed rest."

"I feel it when Mash isn't working at home, and I'm alone for days at a time. Not so much when I was traveling with him. Now you guys are here and we're supposed to be together, but Shannon is off somewhere screwing my new boss."

We laughed out loud.

"But in all seriousness, I haven't made friends with anyone since I've been here. Olive could have potentially become my friend, but Shannon has ruined that from happening."

Khai nodded. "It wasn't intentional though."

"I guess. It's been difficult doing this marriage thing, this handle his ex-girlfriend thing without my friends. My sisters."

"We're just a phone call away. And I think you're handling it just fine. You've grown up since you've been here."

I blushed. "Have any of you figured out what's bothering Taylor?"

"I was hoping you had the *deets* and were about to tell me." Khai played her hand.

"Isla is probably the only one who knows. You should ask her. If not, I will in three weeks when we are all finally back together again."

We played a few more rounds until Shannon strolled in on cloud nine. In the morning we left Paris, forced to listen to Shannon's filthy night throughout the flight. Mr. Hunt chuckled to himself while Shannon's vivid description of her evening entertained and shamed us until we landed back in London.

"If your mother is as lively as you are, tell her I've got a set of wheels to park at her doorstep." Mr. Hunt helped her down the steps.

"I'll pass along the message, but you ain't ready for my mama." Shannon cackled as we said our goodbyes at Heathrow.

"See you in three weeks!"

BRO CODE

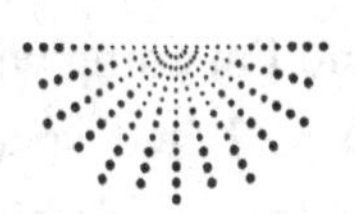

*A*wakened by a kiss in the morning, Mr. Sharper returned from his weekend in Germany. "Morning. Kiss me again." He obliged. "Again." I held his lips longer, and he chortled in my mouth. "Thank you."

"What for?"

"You always smile at me when you come home. Don't ever change that."

He placed fresh orchids at my bedside, removed his coat, and tossed it on the chaise against the wall. With his hands in his pocket, he eyed me from the middle of the room.

"Would you like to go get breakfast, or are you taking the day off?"

I patted the sheets with my palms. "I'd rather lie in bed with you for a few hours."

"Tell me about Paris." He kicked off his shoes.

"The seminar was informative. Then overwhelming. I had a moment of imposter syndrome. Shed a tear. Shannon and Yohan hooked up. Twice. Khai had a blast. Overall, good times. Now come to bed."

While he showered, I wrestled with the idea of telling him about the man placing his arm around my shoulder. It felt like too much to share too soon with the money issue looming over us. I wiggled under his arm when he came to bed and opened my mouth, then shut it when he began to speak.

"Your meeting with Han is tomorrow, correct?"

"Un huh." I hummed.

"I went by the office. And I'm going with you in the morning."

My eyes opened wide as I lied speechless. His arm held me tighter. Without seeing his face, I felt his gaze upon the top of my head.

I deflected. "What happened when you went Vegas?"

"The same stuff that always happens. Money was won, money was lost, clubbing, alcohol at every turn, thieves, and whores in every corner."

"What whores? Did anyone hook up?" I attempted to rise.

"I'm not supposed to disclose such information, Nadia. It's a violation of bro code. But no, not to my knowledge. Why do you ask?" His arm refused to budge.

"Did Levi say anything out of the ordinary?"

Mash loosened his grip around me, and I rolled over to face him. "What's with the inquisition?" He squeezed my nose.

I pushed his hand away from my face. "I think something is up with Taylor. She hasn't been herself since she found out she was pregnant. I thought Levi may have told you if they were still having problems."

"The only thing I remember worth mentioning was something about their honeymoon. Apparently, he read a text message Taylor sent to someone that read she was married now, and to stop contacting her."

I jumped up in the bed. My mouth dropped wide enough for a golf ball to fill a whole in one. My hands covered my chest. "I knew she was being extra. It had nothing to do with being a bridezilla. Her questioning my decision to spend time with you was about her own issues. Now it all makes sense why Levi almost cheated with the girl on his job. He was trying to get back at her."

"Luv, it's none of our business, and they are doing fine now so let it go."

"Do you think he resents her?"

"His words not mine. "If I had seen her text beforehand, I wouldn't have married her." That's all I know. Now let it go."

"What else happened that weekend?"

Mash paused and propped his head on interwoven fingers. I raised my brows at him. He exhaled then smiled as he confessed.

"A few of the guys went heavy on me. Saying shit like I hit the jackpot with you. One claimed he had his eye on you. Another voiced he had an issue with couples like us, but gave me a pass because Levi spoke highly of me."

"Who said that?" My voice heightened.

"Doesn't matter."

"Yes, it does. I bet all of them have slept with a white girl before, but are quick to pass judgement on a *sistah* for stepping outside the color line. Damn double standard assholes." I nestled back in his arms. "Did I mention Olive and I settled our differences?"

"What brought that on?"

I hushed with ease from his question.

"Nad. What aren't you telling me?"

I squirmed in his arms and breezed by the incident, feeding him more of the story where Olive and I bonded. His heart pounded in my ear, and the temperature of his skin rose to a high level of heat.

"What did he look like?" he asked.

"White...around fifty I guess...bald...power suit."

"You can't say I didn't warn you. We'll ride into the city together tomorrow."

Nothing I said mattered at that point. He lifted himself and stretched for his phone, fiddling through his calendar while I rested on his chest. He put on his specks while replying to messages.

I looked up at him. "I accepting your invitation."

"My what?" He beamed with furrowed brows.

I climbed on top of him and placed his phone on the nightstand. "You know what those glasses do to me."

10

YOU, ME, HIM, AND HER

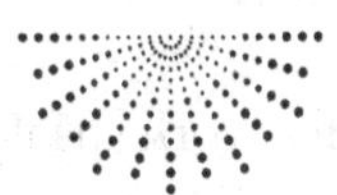

The door closed to the wood-paneled room with Mr. Stallworth and Mr. Sharper on the other side. I sat outside in the hallway pretending to read my drafts, nervous of the discussion on the other side of the wall.

Mash appeared to be in good spirits all morning, but I was worried he would lose his temper when talking with Yohan. I had to trust he wouldn't ruin this opportunity for me, but only time would tell.

The wait was unbearable. After rummaging through everything in my purse, and clockwatching the time on my phone, I paced the hall and settled in an empty room next door to the private meeting amongst men. I spread out my paperwork to review my notes, making out some of the words as the bass of their voices travelled through the thin walls. Moving my chair closer to the air-conditioning vent helped me to better listen in, and as their words became clearer, I caught the tail end of what they were discussing.

When Mash spoke, my body tensed. "Was he at the party?"

Yohan hesitated. "He was on the guest list, but I didn't see him there, and I didn't see what transpired. Olive told me what happened."

"Do me a favor, will you?" The bass in Mash's voice deepened to a new low. "Tell him I know it was him, and I'm not amused."

"Mash, I honestly have no idea who the culprit is. If it were him I would say so, would have spoken up on her behalf had I seen it take place."

"Thank you for making sure my wife will work in a safe environment. She thinks highly of you, ya know. She's super excited for this opportunity."

"She has a fresh voice. Her work speaks for itself."

"On that note, my business here is done. Oh, one more thing before I go. Thank Olive for coming to Nadia's aid for me. It means a lot to the both of us."

"I'll be sure to deliver your message."

"And if you guys want to buy a home from my wife before she commits to this full time, great. But we are doing fine for ourselves and won't be needing any handouts. I believe this belongs to you."

The envelope slapped against the desk and the room fell silent.

"It was good seeing you again, 'Han. We should do this more often. You, me, and the ladies."

"I didn't mean to offend you in any way, Mash." Yohan's voice reeked of stammering guilt.

"You haven't. It was a nice gesture, but we're good. And let's keep everything we've discussed between us? I'll go get Nadia for you."

I rolled back to the table and waited for Yohan's secretary to show the men where I'd wandered. Mash peeped his head into the room.

"I'm done here. Go in there and make magic."

I collected my papers and smiled at him. "Is everything okay?"

He grinned with a twinkle in his eye. "Everything's fine. I'll see you later." He kissed me on the forehead then took off.

The butterflies in my stomach churned when Yohan stood from his desk. I entered the room with a nervous smile, shuddering on the inside.

"I can't believe I'm about to work with you." My voice shook.

"I've wondered for so long how this process works, and now I am about to learn from one of the greats. It's so surreal."

"It's a lot of reading, rewriting, and reshooting, but the hard work pays off. I have my choice for the lead joining us later this week to table read what we come up with today. So, shall we begin?"

For hours we reviewed the original outline while creating a new one, tweaking the dialogue of the first thirty minutes of the film, and discussed different finale scenes to coincide with the meat of the story. Once we wrapped for the day, Yohan questioned my account of the incident.

"It's no big deal," I said.

"It is a big deal, and can become a great deal. I don't want a lawsuit of any kind to damage my company's reputation."

"I would never." I clutched my neck.

"You're not the villain here." He crossed his hands. "I'm just trying to find out who it is, so I can make sure they are aware this type of behavior will not be tolerated. There were several producers, camera men, and casting directors in attendance over the weekend, and it's not the way I run my business."

"Which is why I wouldn't have said anything." I mumbled.

"Which makes it even worse."

"Sure, I was uncomfortable, but it was a split second and I handled it quickly. I thought removing myself from the situation was all I needed to do. Others including Olive saw it happen, so I can't be labeled a liar which is what matters the most to me. I wasn't hurt, and I would like it if we could let it go. Please?"

"Are you sure?"

My shoulders slumped and head dropped. "Yes. I just want to move on and work."

"If you change your mind don't hesitate to speak up." Yohan rose from his seat. "Great work today."

"Thank you. My first day was fun."

"It won't be fun always. You'll see."

Three weeks in and I had yet to see a downside in my new

career, but found frustration searching for land and available lots where Mash and I could build. A change of scenery could only do us some good as we fled dreary London for the states, where my return home was long overdue. If only I had known what I was returning home to.

11

GOIN' BACK DOWN SOUTH

The true meaning of summer as I know it settled on my skin inside the plane before we landed. I could feel the temperature change from the heat seeping through the window, and my infectious smile travelled across Mash's lips. Two years was a long time to be away.

First stop, Taylor's house as a kind gesture since she was unable to fly over with the girls. Lying upright in bed with a swollen belly, and misery on her face, I lied about how pretty she looked. For half a second, she cracked a smile until the pain of her pregnancy wiped it away.

I rubbed her forehead and leaned down to hug her. "Are you sure you're going to make it until Monday."

"I hope not. I'm so uncomfortable right now. But look at you." Taylor grimaced. "You kept your word. I didn't think you were coming in until Saturday."

"I wanted to surprise you. We're spending a few days with my mom and Grams, then we're all yours."

"You should have jumped in here and scared this baby out of me." Her groggy voice grumbled.

"I hate to see you like this, Tay. Have you been like this for the entire pregnancy?" I asked knowing the answer.

She huffed. "Look. As soon as this is over, we are going on a girl's trip. I don't care where. Just take me away."

I grabbed her hand, waiting for a laugh, or any following statement she could offer to clarify her words, but silence bestowed upon us for too long.

"Let's get the baby here first before we start planning your push party. This is supposed to be a happy time, and I for one am ready to meet this baby, and love it, and spoil it."

"Nadia, it's been hell. So many complications. My blood pressure, the preeclampsia, the bed rest, the never-ending worry. Where is Mash?"

"Out back with Levi." My face scrunched. "Bosom buddies."

A second attempt at smiling crossed Taylor's lips. "You know you can make me laugh. How are you two getting along?"

"Good for the most part. We're selling the house and looking to build from scratch. It's stressful, but I'm excited."

"What's wrong with the house I came to?" She grunted, turning to her side in search of comfort.

I adjusted the two pillows propping her up and shrugged my shoulders. "Downsizing feels like the right thing to do. What time do we need to be at the hospital Monday morning?"

"Nine."

"We'll be there. I'm going to let you rest while we get on this road. Call me if anything changes." I tapped her arm.

"Bring me a candy apple back from the shop your grandmother took us to. Please."

Levi and Mash strolled into the room.

"She has been talking about a candy apple for a week now," Levi said, kissing Taylor's forehead.

"How are you feeling Taylor?" Mash asked.

"Like strings are being pulled inside of me. I see you've been taking care of my girl pretty well. She tells me you're selling that monster house."

"We are. Levi has already promised you three will be our first guests like last time."

"All I needed was an invitation." She smirked.

"And I'll see to it you get an apple or two." Mash grinned.

"Thank you." Taylor rolled her eyes at Levi. "Someone in this room wouldn't get me one."

Levi stuttered. "I would have, but she doesn't need it, and she knows it. My job was to make sure the two of them eat healthy and relax."

I interrupted. "Well it's a good thing you won't get it until after the baby is here. We have to get going, but we'll see you guys in a few days."

During the short drive to my mother's house, I realized driving on the wrong side of the road in London had become natural for me. Returning home and driving the way I was taught, the American way, suddenly felt odd until I took a few twists and turns down the interstate.

The arms of my mother felt like warm cushions inside a goose down coat. "So good to see my baby." She repeated numerous times before squeezing the life out of Mash. Her brown skin still glistened, and smelled of Camay and roses, and her joyful tears rolled down her cheeks while singing praises at the sight of us. "I can't believe it's been this long since my baby's been home. I wish you two would stay longer, but I'll take what I can get. My bags are already packed for the morning. You two get on in here and get some rest. We have an early day tomorrow, and I know y'all are tired."

We settled in, reminiscing about the last time we slept in the guest room. Spent from the trip, we fell asleep as soon as we hit the sheets, but recreated the passion years ago in the morning with a good, quick, quiet missionary stroke. I wondered, *'Why does sneaking to make love feel so damn good. Is it the holding of your breath, the risk of being caught, or the forced restriction of my mouth? Note to self, 'Explore this further.'*

I held onto him, feeling the closeness I normally experienced after Mash took care of me. Unfortunately, my comfort and desire to snooze came to a halt once the noise from upstairs, made its way downstairs to wake us up to hit the road.

After two and a half hours of mild South Carolina traffic, we arrived in Goose Creek when the doors opened at the home. I left Mom and Mash chatting with the receptionist, and hurried to Gram's room.

There she sat in her rocking chair, staring out of the window in a comfortable sweat suit, and her hair pulled into a ball behind her ears.

"There is my pretty lady?" I said, as always when entering her room.

Grams jerked and threw her hands. "Why I didn't expect to see you until the party tomorrow." She pulled her fragile body up by the sides of her chair.

"You know how I do." I hugged her tight.

"And I take it my new grandson with the million dollar smile is in the doorway, or is he my birthday present?" She teased.

"Grammy!"

"Hello, I'm Maximus." He kissed the back of her hand. "It's nice to finally meet you."

"Oh no sweetheart, plant me one right here." Grams pointed to her cheek.

"Momma behave." My mother exhaled.

"Now you know I will do no such thing. Nadia baby, you did good I tell you what. Mmm hmm. So handsome."

"I'm thrilled you approve." I tapped her hand.

"Oh yeah. Grams lives on in you my sweet girl." She clutched onto my hand.

"How have you been doing?"

"Really good. Still here to see another birthday."

"How young are you tomorrow, if I may ask?" Mash interrupted.

"80 years young."

"You don't look a day over 50."

"Max baby, when you get tired of this one you give me a call. I'm the original. She's the remix."

"Yes ma'am." His face turned red.

Mom scoffed and grabbed Grams sweater from the closet. "Momma, what do you want to do today?"

"If you're not too tired, I'd like to go for a drive."

"Anywhere in particular?"

"You know the answer without asking."

"By the water." We said simultaneously.

We checked into one of many new hotel chains off the highway, and drove less than an hour to the beach at the Isle of Palms. An immense crowd beat us to the sand, and rented all of the beach chairs and umbrellas. To make the best of the drive, Grams and I held hands walking along the edge of water, sneaking in one of our private chats.

The breeze picked up and nearly carried her away, so we cut our time short on the water, and drove downtown to the city of Charleston for sight-seeing and shopping. For the first time, Mash witnessed the oppressing culture hovering above the city. He questioned the statues of confederate generals, reminiscent of how the good ole boys thought highly of their discriminatory practices. And after learning what took place below the bricks of the market, and the history looming above and below the city, he refused to walk inside of it.

We walked on the pavement parallel to the ghosts of slavery where well to do bakeries, cafes, and souvenir shoppes thrived from the tourism of people who either preserved history, or craved to relive it.

Mash stared at me in a manner he hadn't before. I avoided making eye contact with him, inhaling the smell of fresh pralines as I read his thoughts like a telepath. He had a plethora of questions, but kept them to himself, and I was grateful he knew I didn't want to discuss the past of Charles Town.

We reached the shopping district on King Street which lightened the mood with chain retail stores blended in with mom and pop businesses. The wind blew his hand into mine. He grabbed it and stopped walking until I looked at him, and spoke to me with his eyes. I refused to initiate the conversation he desperately tried to create, and leaned into him, accepting a kiss instead.

Grams spotted a pleated dress in the window of a boutique. Mash bought it for her birthday, along with a necklace, and sun hat for mom. After they were gifted with presents, we walked back towards the depressing side of the city, and grabbed a late lunch.

The freshness of the seafood satisfied our palette. It tasted as if it just came out of the water. We ate ala carte from every dish brought to our table, then headed back to the countryside to retire for the night with to go trays of shrimp, grits, and coconut cake.

Mash bombarded me with the questions and conversation I dodged earlier in the city.

"Have you ever looked up your lineage?" he asked.

"No, and I don't plan on it. I don't trust those DNA sites. My people's history is forever lost so..."

"How do you know it's not accurate?"

"I don't know for sure. It's a feeling I have. I can go as far back as my great-great-grandparents and that's it. Now can we..."

"For both parents?"

"Yes." I sighed. "Can't you tell I really don't want to talk about this."

"Yeah, which makes me wonder why." He moved in close.

"Because it upsets me!"

"It should. It's fucked up. Everything your grandmother taught me today made me think about how Taylor treated me because of the color of my skin. How she still sees me."

"The world has changed since then. We still have a long way to go, but at least you and I can walk hand in hand in public without being thrown in jail."

"It's so bizarre to even think we could have been kept apart. Come here."

I walked over to him staring out of the window. He turned to me and said, "Let the ancestors of this forsaken place watch me kiss you with nothing but love in my heart."

"You're being silly." I stepped away from the window.

He pulled me into him. "I'm being serious. If we lived back then, I'd go to jail for you over, and over, and over."

"You know they would have locked me up too, right?" I looked up at him. "Beat me. Violate me. Kill me."

Mash's face dropped hearing more of the dark history of the south. He closed the drapes, and carried me to the bed still covered in our filth from the day. Slowly, he removed the straps from my dress and caressed me from my hairline to my neck, beautifying every feature his fingers touched. He kissed me until I was covered in the trace of his lips. I trembled from the desire growing inside of me, wanting the animal, having to settle for the gentleman.

He slid inside and turned my face towards him by my chin. "Look at me." I stared into his brown eyes as they told the story of his love for me. "Do you see me?" he asked, stroking me hard before pausing.

"I see you." I gasped softly.

"It's you and me." He repeated over, and over, firmly stroking and pausing deep against the arc of my flesh.

"I know," I said, holding him tightly, failing to hold my breath to sustain the pleasurable pain of his strokes.

Faster thrusts stimulated my zone, then he paused again, holding his schlong in place against the top of my walls.

I squeezed him tight and pled. "Give it to me."

He poked every corner he could touch while his head rested upon my chest and softly whispered, "You're mine."

His grip, firm and perfect, held me close as together we and peaked to our destination. Heavy breaths warmed my chest, then he raised his head. Our eyes met, continuing the tale of affection he housed for me.

Lingering above my face, he brushed my cheek with one hand, and gripped my body with the other. We spoke without words. Bonded by our bodies and souls. Connected by his gratifying caress.

Fatigued and full, I relaxed in his hands, shifting my hips to lie beside him, falling asleep in his embrace, waking hours later still connected in the same position. Naked and cold, I slid from beneath him and maneuvered the comforter to cover us, staring at the ceiling with unimaginable thoughts of what if we were born in a time where our love would have been forbidden.

The thought saddened me into slumber, but I woke with a smile on my face, resting in the arms of love.

The natural alarm clock, also known as my mother, lit a fire under us to begin the day. She and Mash decorated the hall at the home before the guests arrived, while I kept Grams occupied, continuing our talk during a short private stroll around the town.

"Which one of your boyfriends will be at the party today?" I asked.

"Two of them will be there today. But I promised the third one I would save him a piece of cake."

I swallowed my laughter. "Which one do you like the most so I will know what to say?"

"I'm guessing Ernest. He still has his hair." She nodded. "Baby girl, do you have a boyfriend?"

"Grams, don't worry me now. You just spent the day with my husband." I placed the back of my hand under her neck.

"I don't have a fever gal. I know you have a husband. I asked if you have a boyfriend."

"Oh. Um. No. Just the husband."

"Don't be slow gal. Your husband is a good fella, but they can turn on you at any time. Be prepared with a back-up."

"Grammy?"

"Remember my words baby girl. It might not be for twenty years, but there will come a moment when you are going to wish you had someone else who loves you. And waiting for the day you come running."

"Did you wish you had a back-up plan?"

"Wish!" She laughed. "Hell, I had two. My mama told me what I'm telling you. Your mother is the slow one. She loved your father as if there were no other men in the world. Don't get me wrong, your dad was okay. He loved you and was a good provider, but he played out there in them streets, and your mother held her hurt inside and buried it. She had no one to turn to but me. By that time, she didn't know how to be with another man. Then when your father died she just gave up trying. She didn't get that weak shit from me."

"I've told her to get out there and start dating, but she won't do it." I huffed.

"I know. She has so much life left in her, and just wasting it doing nothing, and no one. There's no getting her back in the game." Grams shook her head.

"What do you know about the game?" I chuckled.

"Gal, my generation invented the game."

Sharply at four o'clock, a few family members along with my brother and his wife arrived to the home bearing gifts. We settled in the dining hall alongside Gram's friends from the village, and two of her childhood friends who made a surprise appearance. The look on her face was priceless at the sight of her guests, and there was more life in this room of retirees, than inside a maternity ward.

We listened to the lively bunch of elderly friends tell stories of their youth, share memories about the rebel we were celebrating, and laughed and danced until the moon was above us, and the chirps of grasshoppers drowned us in the garden.

"I see a lot of your grandmother in you." Mash snuck behind me and whispered in my ear. "See how she is so carefree and one with the world?"

"She is amazing, isn't she? Even now in her senior years."

"And so are you." He delicately wrapped his arms around me from the rear.

"Let's not get side tracked. We are supposed to be cleaning up." I squirmed from his embrace.

He reeled me back in and kissed the back of my shoulder. "Why are you running away?"

"Because everyone is staring at us."

"Let them look." He swayed me back and forth.

"The faster we get this stuff up, the faster we can get back to the hotel."

He pecked my lips. "You've won your case."

"Oh, get a room!" Ernest shouted, strolling to his room.

In the morning, we swung by the Sweet Shoppe to grab a few apples for Taylor, then said good-bye to Grams. She promised to get on a plane and visit us, and out of habit slipped Mash a twenty-dollar bill in cash. His face scrunched before he looked at me bewildered.

"Just take it." I mouthed.

He kissed her cheek. "Thank you."

Mash waited until we pulled out of the lot and held up the bill. My eyes met my mothers and we guffawed at the look bridled on his face.

"Why did Grams give me money like a magician?" he asked.

My mother tapped the back of his hand. "It's the way of black grandparents. Their secret passage of giving."

"Did she slip you money, Nadia?"

"We also don't tell anyone if they do."

I watched him grin ear to ear in the rearview mirror, happy to be welcomed as a part of my family. He folded the money like an accordion, tucked it in his wallet, and left it there. He called it his lucky charm.

HURTS LIKE HELL

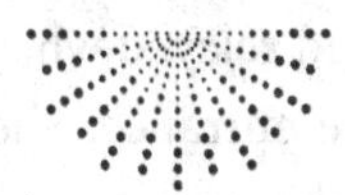

ash stayed behind while I waited with Taylor's family in the waiting room. The grandmothers passed candy back and forth, the grandfathers tapped their shoes on the carpet, and Taylor's mother fiddled with the strap of her purse while her dad eyed the apples in my lap.

He grinned on the side of his mouth, then snuck a few more peeps at the treats. "You're guarding those apples pretty good." He sat back and chuckled to himself.

I smiled at him. "A pregnant lady gets what a pregnant lady wants."

Levi turned the corner. "It's a boy."

His announcement of the moment sounded different than I imagined, then I noticed his hands were trembling, and the look of shock in his eyes.

His mother hugged him. "Son what's wrong?"

A tear fell on his mother's shoulder. "Taylor suffered a light stroke during labor. She's stable and the baby is doing fine." He stuttered.

A collective gasp resounded in our corner.

"I need to be with my daughter." Taylor's mother darted toward the nurse's desk.

Levi broke his mother's hold. "I'll walk you back."

"When can we see the baby?" His mother asked.

"Should be in a few minutes. I'll take you back one at a time once I receive word." He charged after Taylor's mother.

Immediately I texted Mash. '*86 the cigar. I'll explain later. Call you in a few.*' Then, I ran outside and relayed what happened to Shannon and Khai as Isla approached the entrance. She and I surprised everyone with a hug. The news of Taylor's stroke killed the turmoil between us.

The girls went back inside to sit with the family. I hung back for a moment alone, taking deep breaths as I waited for Mash to arrive.

I prayed while I melted under the shade of a tree doing little justice, recalling what I said to Taylor when I first arrived. '*Everything is going to be alright.*' I never imagined the delivery could take such a horrid turn.

The sirens and the birds blended in the background as I cried for my friend's life, watching cars come and go in a daze. Loud music blasted from a car backing into a space in the lot. I turned towards it, catching a clear view of the car parked in the space next to it. The silhouette of the owner's head was easily recognizable. I walked over to the vehicle and knocked on the glass. "Dylan?"

He lowered the window, halfway revealing his perfect teeth and scruffy goatee. A few white specks had sprouted in his beard, but he looked exactly as I remembered. Still good looking. Still lust worthy.

"It's been a long time Nadia. How are you?"

"It has been a long time. Pardon me for asking, but what are you doing sitting out here?"

"I'm waiting for someone to come out. Life's been good to you I see." He squinted his smoldering eyes, and fully smiled this time. "You still look the same Cocoa Queen."

I pretended hearing his nickname for me didn't make me a little wet. I scoffed. "I forgot you called me that." I fought to hide any sight of blushing.

"You're still pretty when you cry. What's wrong?"

He still had a way of making me blush with a simple compliment, and tone that mocked he cared. Hearing him say those words made me wonder if that was part of the reason he kept me in tears for all of those years.

"I just got some bad news. You remember my friend, Taylor?"

"Of course, I do."

"She just gave birth and suffered a stroke."

"Aw man. Is she alright?" His grin disappeared.

"She's stable, and the baby is fine. It's just sad and unexpected you know." I wiped my eyes. "Actually, I should get back inside."

"I'm sorry to hear about your friend. I hope she pulls through. It was good seeing you Cocoa Queen. I heard you got married, and live out of the country now. You're big time huh?"

I pressed my lips together then parted my lips. "And I couldn't be happier."

"You look happy, besides the pretty tears. You take care of yourself."

I walked back inside with my head held high. I hadn't missed anything when it came to Dylan. Same old Dylan. Same old story. Vague in his responses, and elusive in answering questions. To think once upon a time I thought the world of him. The times had changed, and favor was on my side.

While waiting for Mash to arrive, I held Levi's hand for a moment. "Do you want to see the baby?" he asked.

I clutched his hand. "Of course, I do."

He showed me to the washroom where we covered in blue paper cloth gowns. The wet nurse opened the door to the baby ward where four new souls had been brought into the world. A boisterous baby girl broadcasted her presence as we entered, bringing a smile to my face. Next to her was the cutest baby I ever laid eyes on.

He had a head full of hair which explained Taylor's indigestion, big sweet cheeks, and pouting lips.

"Am I allowed to pick him up?" I asked.

The nurse nodded yes.

Immediately, I inhaled the sugary scent of sweetness, innocence, and new life. A smell so special it has yet to be duplicated.

"Levi, I'm in love. What's his name?"

"Tyler, after his mother. I wanted to name him LJ after me, but of course his mother always gets her way."

"Either name would have been perfect like him."

"Thanks, Nadia."

"My flight leaves Wednesday night, but say the word, and I'll change it."

"I know you would, but we have more than enough family to help us out."

"When can I see Taylor?"

"They are saying only family can go back, so I'll tell them you're her sister. All of you will get the green light."

"We love you both, and are here for whatever you need." I squeezed his shoulder.

The waiting room was packed when we returned from the baby ward. One by one we took turns visiting Taylor's bedside. Mash checked on Levi, taking him outside for a breather away from the billion questions and commotion, and with the coast being clear, I filled the girls in on my parking lot coincidence.

"I ran into Dylan outside," I blurted, twisting my mouth.

"Oh shit." Isla mumbled.

"Of all days," said Shannon.

"Of all places." Khai added. "You okay?"

"Yeah. It was—well—it was fine. And brief. He said he was waiting on someone. And that was it."

"Do you think someone told him you were here, and he was out there hoping to see you?" Khai asked.

"I didn't get the sense he cared he ran into me."

"There is a GOD. That chapter is actually over." Shannon held her hands in prayer pose.

"That chapter was over when I dipped my toes in the waters of Lake Minnetonka."

My joke went over well, causing a stir that had to be silenced when Taylor's parents came back into the room. Isla jumped up and asked to join Levi's mother to visit Taylor next.

Shannon waited for Isla to leave, then whispered, "I'm proud of you girl. I thought you would fall back into your old ways if you ever saw Dylan again. That hold on you was strong." She fanned herself.

"I'm actually glad I ran into him. There were no fantasies of running off into the sunset with him, or anything. I got to see that I traded up." I smiled.

Khai chimed in. "Under normal circumstances, this would have been a reason to go out and celebrate, but..."

"It's not that big of deal, really. Just a little weird because it's like I felt closure, but I should have had closure before I married another man, right?"

"Usually. But in your case, you get to be an exception." Khai chuckled, tapping my leg.

It was soon my turn to visit Taylor. Seeing her unconscious, hooked up to machine after machine, and swollen with tubes attached to her body was surreal. I held one hand and Khai held the other, while we talked to her, knowing she could hear us and feel our presence.

Khai brushed her hair and braided it down, while I skimmed through the cards and flowers. One after the other, I read the kind words people wrote to her, hoping she would flinch from the overwhelming love she received. Unfortunately, it was I who flinched, as I read aloud one of the most beautifully written cards in the pile. My eyes jumped out of my head, and my chest concaved at the signature. *Dylan.*

Khai glared at me as I stared at Taylor. "Did you just say what I think you said?"

I was speechless. My pores felt wide open and my eyes saw red. Old feelings stirred in me, and I panicked, breathing as though I was the one who needed to be hooked up to the machines.

"He must have sent those after you talked to him outside?" Khai suggested

I shrugged my shoulders. "I'm going to call it a day and let someone else visit."

She pressed on my heels. "Nadia."

"I'm fine." I escaped to the parking lot.

Khai followed me closely.

"His car hasn't moved." I groused. "He said he was waiting for someone to come out. He meant he was waiting for Levi to leave, so he could go in."

"You're reaching, Nadia. It's all speculation." Khai chastised me. "You're letting your emotions get the best of you because it is Dylan we are talking about. He has always brought out the worst in you."

"Khai. I'm about to break my wife code and tell you something. When the guys were in Vegas, Levi told Mash Taylor was seeing someone up until the wedding. She sent a breakup text to someone on their honeymoon. That's why they've been fighting so much since the wedding."

"Brian didn't tell me about this."

"And I promised Mash I wouldn't say anything either. But now I've told you. That message was sent to Dylan. I know it. Think about how erratic she acted when Mash and I met. She questioned us being in love, and so into each other. My finding someone better pissed her off because she could no longer hold her little secret over my head."

"Speculation. Our friend needs us right now. I won't be a part of this. You can stand out here by yourself, and have a mental break-down about a sketchy ass ex-boyfriend. Snap the fuck out of it." Khai snapped her fingers in my face. "Check yourself before you come back in."

Once Khai disappeared, I left a note on Dylan's car with the words, 'I know the truth.' I walked amongst the heavy traffic, and returned to the entrance when Mash texted he was looking for my whereabouts.

He met me outside and held me tight. His strong arms squeezed the frustration from my bones, assuring me everything was going to be okay, and assuming I was upset at Taylor's condition.

As I clung to him, confused and outraged, I spotted Dylan strutting to his car. I watched him read my note, and our eyes met while I was in Mash's arms. His shoulders sunk and he exhaled as I death stared him until he drove away.

I kept my cool by leaving the hospital. Betrayal at the hands of two people I loved ran circles around me, but somehow, I found the strength to return the next afternoon.

The commotion died significantly, so I was able to visit Taylor without waiting. I sat next to her, pouring my heart out of the pain she had caused me, hoping she heard every word I spoke.

I took a breather and spent time with the baby in the nursery as others stopped by to visit her, and returned once the

room had cleared. The nurse wheeled in her son, and I fed him for her, laid him on her chest for a few minutes so she could feel him near her, then read to Taylor after the nurse took Tyler away for his bath.

In my final hour of visitation, Dylan strolled in the room. I wrestled with having him thrown out. He knew from the look in my eyes he wasn't wanted, but before I could part my lips to lash into him, he sat opposite me across the bed.

"I wasn't expecting to see you on yesterday." He sighed. "I didn't know what to say."

The nurse rolled the baby back into the room. "He's already been fed, and is talking quite a bit tonight. I thought she might want to listen to him. I'll be back for him shortly."

I walked over to the sink to wash my hands, then picked up the baby from his crib. Like before, I laid him on his mother's chest, cooing and giggling.

Dylan stood and placed his hand on Tyler's back. "Have they said how long she will be in here?"

"No. They don't know yet. Do you think it's wise for you to be here?" I held Tyler back in my arms.

"Nadia." Dylan hummed.

"Don't."

"Let me explain."

I cut him off. "You know I always wanted to hold your baby in my arms. And look at me. I am. Not the way I imagined it, but here I am. Funny isn't it."

"We never messed around while you and I were together."

"Am I supposed to say thank you? Like what is your purpose in life? To go around and ruin people's lives? I mean you messed me up for years. Had me wondering why I wasn't good enough. What did I do to make you not love me? Or pretend to love me and waste my time? I prayed for God to fix whatever was wrong with me so you could love me. And when you didn't, I compared every man I dated to you. Trying to measure up to this false image I had given you. Now I see how stupid I was. You're worthless. And now here we are. Seven years later, and you are still doing the same old bullshit. You've ruined my relationship with my best friend. Do you know that? Probably ruined her marriage to a good man, too. He so doesn't deserve this shit. And now there's this innocent baby caught in the middle— of your shit."

Typical Dylan ignored my spill. "Can I hold my son?" He reached for the baby.

I gasped and held Tyler closer to me. "Your son. Ha! This baby's last name is Fields."

"Nadia, please. I came when Levi left so there wouldn't be any trouble." His hands twanged.

"But you're the trouble. Don't you see that?"

"Just let me hold him for one second." He begged.

The desperation in his eyes made me feel sorry for him. My pity overpowered the hate I felt for him. My love for Levi forbade me to place Tyler in his arms. "I'm going to put him in his crib and get the nurse. What you choose to do when I leave is on you."

I lied. I never went to get the nurse. I stood at the corner of the room, and monitored them through the blinds. Dylan picked up Tyler, and kissed his forehead, studying his features. As he searched for himself in the baby's beauty, he mouthed something in his ear, then placed him back into the crib. Tyler's finger wrapped around his when he laid him down, then he kissed him once more before hovering over Taylor. He kissed each of her cheeks, then her lips, and slowly exited the room looking back at her and the baby.

Upon his exit, our paths crossed one last time. With what resembled remorse written on his face he said, "I'm sorry."

I held back my tears in front of him, but bawled in silence after the nurse wheeled Tyler away. Before Levi arrived, I cleaned my face. He walked in as I was squeezing Taylor's hand. I hugged him goodbye before he stepped outside the room with the nurse for an update. Then I whispered in Taylor's ear, "I hope you wake up soon and find peace." And I left her and my past behind.

13

TILL FOREVER FALLS APART

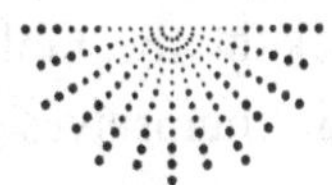

*I*t was easy to mask my hurt as sadness. Mash comforted me for days, tending to my needs and walking on eggshells as he patiently waited for the day a smile would return to my face. I grew restless tussling with the idea of fessing up the bombshell that dropped in my lap, but I feared the validation of my anger would be dismissed, and thought it was best to keep him in the dark, out of respect for his friendship with Levi.

Ruining Levi and Mash's bromance was at risk, so for weeks I carried the burden of truth on the edge of my tongue. The load was so heavy I could barely think straight, until I buried myself into my work.

I spent most of my time focusing on the film, viewing audition tapes, meeting with actors, and sitting in on the selection process. I neglected helping with the plot search, and shut off communication across the pond with everyone in Charlotte. Then, the universe decided to throw me a curve—

Olive invited me out for drinks.

Red always had my name on it, but I became obsessed with a cocktail Olive introduced to me called a lime elderflower. I ordered a second with appetizers, and as the hours went by I felt the most relaxed I had since returning from the states.

Early evening became night, and the night became my bitch. We were having too much fun to go home, so we went to a nightclub where we skipped the line thanks to her clout. I danced like I did the first night I arrived in London, except this time I was too inebriated to engage in a battle.

I ruffled my blouse back at the table. Some young boys sent drinks over and took it upon themselves to sit with us. I engaged in a game of flirtation with the cutest one until he turned creepy, studying my wedding band like a thief.

He gripped my hand. "What say we give the old ball a break tonight. Come back to my place, and decide in the morning if you want to leave," he whispered in my ear.

"Wow. I must really look tanked." I slowly pulled my hand away.

"Hot is more on the lines of what I was thinking." He winked.

Olive realized the heat was rising and our company was getting too comfortable. We shared a look, reading each other's minds, then she improvised.

"Sorry to end the party boys, but we've entertained you long enough. We can't be seen fraternizing with patrons all night long."

The boys laughed in a threatening tone, then the cute one sitting next to me said, "Who the fuck are you to call us patrons?"

Olive raised her glass and saluted the owner standing on the podium near the stage. Within minutes, he and a bouncer appeared at our table.

"Baby, my friend and I were just leaving. See to it these gentlemen receive a drink on the house." She looked both of the boys in the eyes. "Thanks for keeping us company."

The club owner escorted us safely to the exit, whispered something in Olive's ear, then passed us over to Yohan's driver, Mervin. Laughing hysterically like idiots, we hopped in the back of the car.

"That was brilliant back there. I was starting to get scared." I confessed.

"I picked up on a weird vibe with those two. Just goes to show you, looks aren't everything. The one talking in your face was cute, but had a temper. I sensed it when you turned him down. But enough about those losers, did you have a good time tonight?"

"A great time. You have no idea how much I needed this." I slurred, leaning against the door.

"I meant to call you sooner, but my schedule was full. I'm glad I ran into you today." Olive smiled to herself.

"The stars aligned for us to hang out. My plans for the evening were to drop by the radio station, and watch my husband host his guest spot."

"Is he still there?" Olive's face stiffened suddenly.

"I don't know. Can you ask Mervin to turn to 98.9?"

"I can do better than that. Mervin…"

"I'm on it, Ms. Lapois." He tipped his hat.

The car exited the ramp blasting the techno music in session at the studio. The bass thumped through the speakers in the trunk, and I zoned out waiting to hear Mash's deep voice speak to his audience. *Speak to me.*

Moments later he announced the artists he collaborated with on the song.

"That's my baby! Mmm, he's gonna get it tonight!" I shouted.

"You're so in love it makes me nauseous." Olive fanned her hands. "Look at you. You're smiling all goofy. I didn't believe real love still existed in this new age. You two are the exception."

"Yet you find us nauseating?" I frowned.

"I saw you two together a few years back in Cannes. I'm sure you know interracial couples stick out more than most, but what was eye catching was how protective he was of you. I also saw you in the hallway the day of your first meeting with Yogi. He walked you in. Kissed you on the forehead. Hesitated to leave."

"He did?"

"Yes, he did. I thought to myself, *'Damn, she has him hooked.'* But in all seriousness, what did you do to him?" Olive encouraged me with her eyes.

I chuckled to myself and hid my face beneath my palms. "I wish I knew. We had a surreal connection from day one, and here I am. I couldn't have found a better man to love me."

Olive scoffed. "I learned the hard way, it is better for a man to love you more than you love him."

"Oh my God Olive! You would get along great with my grandmother. She'd be so proud if she heard you say that."

The song on the radio neared the end and the beat continued to play. My eyes grew big, then I buried my face into my hands.

"What's wrong?" Olive asked.

I shrieked. "I can't believe he's going to play this entire song. I'm so embarrassed."

The tagline streamed and Mash's voice lit the airwaves. "Sup, Nad."

Olive's mouth dropped. "Is that you?"

I nodded. "I can't believe he played that on the radio."

Olive cackled. "See what I mean— love."

I blushed all the way to the station. Olive and I ended the night on a high with a hug.

"We have to do this again, Nadia."

"Most definitely. I haven't made any friends since I've moved here. You have no idea how much tonight meant to me."

"I'm not sure what kind of drinker you are, but I'm taking a cycle class in the morning. I'll send you the address. If I see you there, great. If not, I'll know you can't handle your liquor." She laughed.

"Well I guess you'll find out in the morning."

I went inside the studio of the radio station and watched Mash work through the glass. Something about the way he looks at me down his nose when he's working gets me going—

His hands mixing, his head held high, looking down at me with sexual energy while I was heavily liquored up made his gaze even more enticing. I could see us checking into a hotel in the city just to get one good fuck in.

Incessant calls from Shannon and Khai buzzed in my purse as I was daydreaming how I would jump my husband's bones. I sent their calls to voicemail, then was hit with urgent texts until I silenced my phone.

Mash stumbled into me. "You reek of prosecco. I take it this wasn't a red wine kind of night?" He smirked and held me close.

"Nope." I slurred. "Olive turned me onto something new."

"Olive?"

"Yeah, we hung out after we wrapped tonight. Turns out she's a fun girl."

"I see. Whatever you two got into worked. You seem lighter than you have been these past few weeks. Is everything okay now?"

"I don't know if things will ever be okay? Hey, I was thinking we could get a room in the city tonight and you know..." I purred, leaning on him.

"I'd rather get you home and give you what you're asking for. We have something to celebrate." He teased me with pecks on my cheek.

"What?"

"We were approved to buy three lots in Richmond. We can start building right away."

"So, it's time to put the Sor Fale sign up. I mean For Sale sign up."

"Wow." Mash snickered. "You are sauced tonight."

The spearmint in his cologne pervaded the car. Lost in his essence, I unbuttoned my blouse, and stopped him from cranking the ignition.

"Come on. Let's get the first one out right now." I begged.

He blew me off, then proceeded to leave the lot with a wrinkled face and sighed. "What's going on with you? And before you say nothing, I want you to know Levi told me you haven't called to check on them once since we left. Something's up. What is it?"

I hyperventilated at the salacious details about to pour from lips and yelled. "I found out Taylor was seeing my ex and he's Tyler's father!"

Mash's face stoned. "Why would you be worked up about her infidelity? I'm hearing you cut everybody off. Even Khai."

"This response is exactly why I kept my mouth shut. No one is going to see my side in this. Taylor was and is still fucking my ex-boyfriend."

"So, you've been sulking about him this whole time?!"

"God no! I'm not mad about him! I'm pissed at Taylor for stabbing me in the back all of these years. And I'm mad at Khai for not believing me, even though I read her the proof. You know I understand Isla doing what she did, but never imagined Taylor would be a throw them in the yard friend."

"A what?"

"It's when women don't trust other women around their man. Where I'm from the rules are don't come to my house if I'm not there. If you need to return something, throw it in the yard and keep it moving."

Mash snorted and choked in the same breath. "Is drunk Nadia making shit up?" He taunted me. "And who originated this rule?"

"I learned it from my Grams."

His mouth opened slightly followed with a grin. "Makes sense. What is Shannon?"

"Throw them in the yard." I scowled at him and my voice deepened.

"And Khai?"

I smiled. "I Trust."

His head leaned back. "Isla?"

"Don't even throw them in the yard, just keep it." I emphasized, turning up my lips and shaking my head side to side.

"Nadia, do you still have feelings for your ex-boyfriend?"

"No. I used to love him. I thought he was the one. And all of the girls knew it. They also knew how much he made me cry. How he killed my self-esteem. How bad he hurt me. I shared everything about our relationship with them. My so-called sisters."

"What am I missing here? You are married to me. Why would Taylor hooking up with your loser ex-boyfriend bother you?"

"There is a code amongst girlfriends. You don't have relations with your best friend's husband, boyfriend, or ex-boyfriend. Period."

"So, everyone in your past is off limits?"

"Yes."

"You're insane." He preached.

"So, hypothetically speaking, if we broke up and Prano asked me out. How would you feel?"

"I wouldn't like it, but there isn't anything I could do about it. I'd probably want to bash in his head, maybe even try, but I wouldn't because you two are consenting adults."

"I call bullshit."

"You're right. I'd hate you and probably kill him."

Hate was a strong word, but my inebriated mind, and sexual hunger ignored his response. I ran straight to the kitchen scouring through the snacks, munching on potato chips while the leftovers warmed in the microwave. Mash surprised me from behind and pinned me to the wall.

"Oh, now somebody wants a piece of me." I teased.

He lifted my top. "I always want a piece of you. If I could, I would relive our first time against this very wall." He pulled on my neck with his mouth.

"Selling the house has you feeling nostalgic?"

"Perhaps," he said, leading me to the floor.

Instead of standing this time, he sat me on his face while he lied on the floor, and sucked me like I was a peach. My eyes rolled back noticing the chip in a cabinet near the floorboard, then my attention diverted back to his elevated foreplay.

I rode him from above, delighted by the french kisses delivered below my crevice until it became too much, then rose to my feet and attempted to flee for a breather. He grew further enticed by the cat and mouse game I was playing, and caught me by my hair, lifting me to the wall.

"You miss this wall, too, don't you?" He grinned ear to ear, and then repeated those magical words from two years prior. "Breathe."

I softly gasped, grabbing on to the back of his head, listening to my body being plowed into the sheet rock as he plunged in my pussy going straight for the kill. Back to back I came, gyrating uncontrollably, causing him to celebrate himself with a cocky smirk.

He owned me. He knew he owned me. He knew I was his, and he was toying with me to satisfy his ego.

Suddenly, he exited my loins and led me to the pool table in the dining room. I expected him to position me the same as before, so I placed my foot in the socket. He laughed devilishly and turned me around. "You remembered, but we're making a new memory tonight." My chest pounded with wonder and my swollen womb throbbed, wanting him to get on with it.

Slow and steady he kissed me before elevating me onto the green velvet. "Lie back," he ordered. I did as I was told, and shivered at the touch of his hands caressing each foot before spreading them apart across the table. "Stay just like that," he commanded.

"What are you doing?"

"I'm going to score this eight ball in your pocket."

"What?"

"You know I wouldn't hurt you. Do you trust me?" He convinced me with hypnotizing eyes.

"I have in the past, but this…"

"I need to hear you say you trust me." He sharpened the bow.

I shivered. "Okay— I trust you."

Commanding and creative suited Mr. Sharper— what I like to call him when he took charge, which was often. I shuddered at the placement of the black and white ball atop the green. Trembling head to toe with my nook spread eagle, I exhaled and studied the flickering light in the fixture. *'What the fuck am I doing'* I thought to myself foolishly staying put.

He leaned down with his pointer in hand and positioned himself to strike the ball. Deeply I gulped, waiting to hear the clank of the ball in pursuit towards my brim, then flinched once it softly tapped me. The anticipation and sensation of the pat aroused me. "Ah." I expelled.

He climbed on the table. "What were you expecting?"

I opened my mouth to answer.

He placed his finger on my lips. "Why would I hurt that beautiful clit," he said, rubbing the ball against my soaked folds in circles.

"What the fuck are you doing to me!" I screamed, staining the velvet.

His dick stood fully erect and he drew himself down, placed his weapon back inside of me, and moaned at touch of my drip surrounding him. "I've dreamed of doing this to you, but never got around to it," he said, tonguing my neck and pulling my hair towards the carpet. The pace of his ride rendered me speechless. I was in full-fledged fuck me mode, mentally traveling into another dimension from the pillage of the beast staking claim on my body.

The only sounds to part my lips were those of gratification, which prompted him to thrust deeper and harder. "What's his name?" He dug inside of me.

I returned back to my reality. "What?" I asked, in between sighs of penetrable passion.

"What's his fucking name?" he asked again.

I raised my head, grabbed his face, and looked into his eyes. "His name is Maximus."

"His name is what?" He stroked firm and hard.

"Maximus!" I shrieked, weakened and eroticized.

"La petite mort." He groaned, clinching me tight as he released his load, blending it with mine.

Lifeless I laid beneath him, panting for uncounted minutes, and faded by his performance. I knew he was speaking French, but I didn't bother to ask what he said. Whatever it was I assumed meant something good, parallel to how I felt buried below him.

Somehow, he found the strength to rise, and pulled the half of my body hanging off of the green onto the table. He disappeared into the kitchen, and returned with the plate of food from the microwave I heated when we arrived home. We devoured the leftovers in all of our nakedness, silent and spiritually in sync. Words weren't need. Only the two of us. Properly fucked and coexisting.

14
GIRLFRIEND

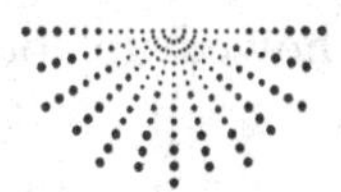

Soul cycle was not the best choice for an amateur drinker of the elderflower like myself. Instead of being true to the current withered state I woke up in, I chose to leave the comfort of my bed to impress Olive as if I had something to prove.

I finagled from under Mash's arm, and promised to cook brunch when I returned from my mission to impress Ms. Perky Slim Jim across town.

It was obvious Olive handled her liquor better than me. I struggled to keep up, and regretted every minute of the tortuous class, while she peddled like a biker in the Tour D' France.

I wondered if she knew I was dying on my bike, and secretly reveled on the inside at my hideous attempt to keep up with the class. I counted the minutes until quitting time, and when the trainer congratulated us for completing our session, I was the first to stop peddling, and curled up in a ball on the floor.

"No time for naps newbie. Let's grab a coffee next door before the crowd beats us." Olive slapped my ass and held out her hand.

I grunted in agony lifting myself from the floor, and followed her next door. She ordered our drinks while I snagged us a table, just in time to beat the rush of other cyclers who took time to shower in the facility.

"I have to be honest with you Olive, I can't wait to crawl back into my bed." I sipped the sugar free brew, nearly gagging when I swallowed. "You're going to be that size forever, aren't you?"

Olive laughed. "Sugar is not your friend."

"It is where I'm from." I cringed at a second sip.

"I was surprised you showed up today. I could tell you were sloshed last night."

"I mainly drink red wine, but I did like whatever flower power you ordered me."

"Yes, the elderflower is amazing. I should have stopped you, but you appeared to enjoy it, and I sensed you needed to release some tension. Is everything going okay with the documentary?"

"So far, so good. Did Yohan put you up to this? I did mention I haven't made any friends here in our conversations."

"No, not at all. When I got in last night he wasn't too thrilled about our little flirtation at the club."

"Our, you say?" We giggled. "You were brilliant by the way."

"Those chums were going to babysit us all night. And the owner and I used to— well you can imagine. He was eyeing us all night, so I knew we were safe. I also knew word about my being there would get back to Yogi. Nothing wrong with a little shameless flirting to keep your man on his toes." She smirked.

Bravely, I sipped the unsweetened beans and studied the vindictiveness in Olive's eyes. *'She's not a slow one,'* I gathered.

I waited for her to stop smiling to herself and admitted. "I haven't flirted with a man since I met my husband."

"Well last night proved you haven't lost your touch. I worry I will lose my game with marriage. How much of myself do I have to give up? Like catching the eye of a man to know I'm still a catch. And the trust." She exhaled deeply. "I struggle with trust. Marriage is so different nowadays. Any advice before I walk the plank?" She raised her brows.

"I love being married. It's not easy every day, but I'm happy most days. Especially knowing Mash has my back and is protective of me. Are you having doubts about the wedding? Sorry to pry."

"I'm having doubts about everything lately. How long were you two together before you trusted him?"

I threw her off with a shy laugh and snort. "Trust is not my strong suit, and we aren't ones to follow rules by any means. We kissed on the first night, didn't hook up the second night because he had to work, and fucked like maniacs the third night. I stayed shacked up with him for three days straight, ignored all of my plans, dismissed my friends, and moved in with him after seven days. I don't know if it was love or lust, but after three months we were married."

"Wow. I mean damn. I mean whoa. Three months and married. And you're happy?" Her voice rose slightly in denial. "I assumed you were long distance lovers or something. Do you have to do special things to keep him interested?" She asked below her breath.

"No. We go at it pretty good." I chortled, thinking of last night.

Olive stirred her drink in a daze. "My concern is will I be enough? So many of my friends say things like they have to have threesomes to please their mate. Or they have these arrangements like one weekend out of the year they get to be single."

"Oh hell no. I'm not with the hall pass life. It can lead to getting you dicmatized or traumatized."

"Exactly. What is the point of being married if you have to do such things? I'm hoping he's getting all of his cheating out of his system now." She sighed.

"Why do you think he's cheating on you?"

"Men like him always cheat."

"Then why marry him?"

"Why not?"

I was stumped. And cornered. And suspicious. *'Did she know about Shannon and thought liquoring me up would make me blab?'* I wondered.

Our conversation paused nearly a minute when I blurted, "I am coming up blank with an answer to your question. I got nothing."

She laughed at my American use of language. "It's fine. My question was rhetorical. Sort of." she shrugged. "I've done well in my career and still turn heads. I'll always end up on the right side with Yohan Stallworth, or another like him. A girl can dream that caliber of a man would be monogamous. But it doesn't exist."

The acceptance of secret affairs in Olive and Yohan's relationship reminded me love, honor, and truth isn't a factor for everyone. Money, status, and security played a huge part in some unions, and seeing the pain in her eyes she thought she was hiding made me grateful I had companionship and love in mine.

"I have a friend whose motto is until she says I do, she is free to spread it around."

"And what about after?"

"Then she'll be faithful. So she says."

"You know I thought about travelling down memory lane last night. If you weren't with me, I might've evened the score." Olive blushed.

"Well, if you listen to my friend's advice, you're free to do as you wish." I sipped my final taste of the bitter coffee.

"I'm so glad we took the time to get to know one another. I have friends, but none of them are this easy to talk to."

"I couldn't agree more. My friends back home aren't thrilled about me finding new friends. They think I'll replace them."

"Come to this luncheon I'm having. I want you to meet my girlfriends. They can sometimes be real bitches, which is why I can't talk to them like this, but you'll fit right in."

I seriously doubted I would fit right in with a group of girls who she considered to be bitchy, but I accepted the invitation graciously.

"Sounds like a plan." I looked at the time on my phone. "I promised the hubs I'd make brunch, so I'm going to head home and feed my man." I rose from the table, startled by Olive's arms wrapping around me.

"It was a pleasure hanging out with you. I'll be in touch soon." She released me. "Ciao."

* * *

MASH WAS STILL ASLEEP when I returned home. I showered, then curated a brunch of his favorite dishes: a Dutch-oven blueberry pancake, country-fried potatoes, and cheese scrambled eggs.

I surprised him with breakfast in bed, waking him with the aroma of confection on the tray. He rubbed his eyes a few times before opening them fully, then smiled at the smell of heaven at his fingertips.

"To what do I owe the pleasure?" he asked.

"You were magnifique last night."

"Was I?" He reached for the fork.

"I like when you get creative."

He smirked. "If it gets me breakfast in bed, I'll defile you more often."

I playfully shoved him and he hid the grin on his face, exposing his mouth full of food.

He swallowed. "How was your workout?"

"Brutal."

"And Olive?"

"She's good. She opened up a little more today."

"Your first friend abroad." His brows raised, looking up at me.

"And perfect timing, too."

"Speaking of friends, Levi messaged again wanting to know why you're being distant. We need to get our stories straight."

I nodded. "Did I answer your question last night?"

He licked his fingers and exhaled as his eyes bounced between me and the plate. "Yeah."

I leaned forward and kissed his sticky lips. "Good."

We lied around for most of the afternoon, me in a t-shirt and no panties, him shirtless in briefs. By evening, my peace was disturbed with a phone call from Khai. Mash insisted I answer.

"It's nice to know you can still hold a grudge," she said.

"Ha ha."

"How are you?"

"At peace."

"So, we're down to short answers. I'd expect nothing less, than for you to make this hard for me. I thought you should know Taylor is recovering well, and hammering me about why you haven't called them. I don't know what to say to her."

"You can tell her I wish her well in all of her future endeavors."

"Nadia. I'm not saying that. What's up with you? You haven't contacted any of us, and yes it has been discussed."

"Because I was right, and you didn't have my back. You always have my back."

"Taylor literally had a stroke. Some things have precedence. Not some wild theory about who is seeing who."

"Well he came to the hospital before my flight, confessed about the affair, and the baby. I'm sure Taylor knows exactly why I haven't called by now. She should be thanking me for getting rid of the evidence before Levi arrived."

"My God. How do we fix this?"

"My friendship with Taylor is over."

"Unacceptable. We are too close for a jackass like Dylan to come between us."

"You know what plays over in my head. How fake she's been to my face. Throwing up the fact I couldn't get over him all these years and she's been fucking him the entire time. What kind of friend does that, Khai?"

Khai sputtered. "Come home. All of us need to hash this out. Face to face. At least come and see the baby. I know you love the baby."

I hung up emotionally drained after declining the request to come home. I sat on the sofa looking at the television on mute without realizing Mash had been watching me sulk. Also, listening to my conversation. I jumped at the sound of his voice.

"I overheard everything. Don't spend too much time being angry. And don't write your friends off just yet."

"Humph. Before we came to London, I broke up with the man Isla is currently dating. That very same night Taylor made me the brunt of her jokes, teasing I was still hung up on my ex, and all of my friends sided with her. All the while she was shagging him, and laughing in my face. Look at it from where I'm sitting. Do you understand how I feel, now?"

"Believe it or not. I do." He joined me on the couch. "Will this affect my friendship with Levi?"

"I hope not. Let's aim to get him in the divorce."

He brushed my cheek, and I captured his hand pressed against my shoulder. He finally understood I was mourning the loss of my friend and my pride, not the dreaded ex. But he was right, I didn't need to spend any more time being angry, when I could be living. And that was exactly what I planned to do.

15

LIGHTS, CAMERA, ACTION

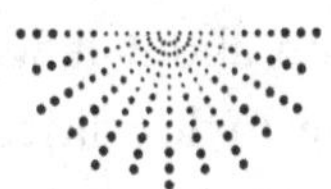

Set life was intimidating. Experienced professionals and production teams ran circles around me in the fast paced, overwhelming, high stressed environment, but as time went on and the more I became familiar with the crew, the long days stopped feeling like work.

I shadowed Yohan closely, following his direction of repetitious orders and demands. Some days went long into the night, pushing Olive and I to spend more time together grabbing dinners and after hour drinks. Sometimes we joined the cast and crew on their late-night antics to the pub down the block. In doing so, the actors became approachable, and in turn I took notice of Chili, a thespian from the U.S. with a huge fan base.

Chili was sweet, fun, and full of life onset. One of the few men who held the door open for women, and made everyone laugh in between takes. He was often seen rehearsing lines to himself in a corner, or openly changing his shirt at the end of scenes. The ladies on set found him very easy on the eyes, and lingered around in-between takes to catch a glimpse of his abs and country boy smile. There was no doubt in my mind he knew what he was doing.

I was shocked to find myself watching him closely during his shirt changes as well. Maximus was hotter than him, and the only vanilla babe I'd ever been attracted to. So, to notice the American boy in such a way made me question if the blue-eyed cutie had come into my world as a test of temptation, or was I now an official hummus shopper?

Moments like this made me miss the girls. Once upon a time I would have ran to them with such gossip, taken the dozen jokes thrown at me, and thought nothing of it. Now, I found myself wondering if I should gossip about it with Olive instead, or apply the lesson I learned from the Taylor fiasco and keep it to myself.

A minor scene didn't receive Yohan's approval. "This looks weak." He complained. "Nadia, stand alongside Chili so we can wrap up this segment tonight." I shook my head no. He leaned over and whispered, "Word of advice, never say no when something needs to be done on your own project, or to the director."

"I'm not an actress, Han. I'm shaking right now. And I don't have on makeup."

"Your back will be facing the camera. Grace! Nadia is standing in as an extra next to Chili. Back facing the camera on the right side of the table."

Grace positioned me on the set.

Yohan screamed. "Roll'em!"

My legs trembled beneath me.

"My God. Stop shaking." Chili mumbled.

I froze and couldn't speak.

"Breathe," he said.

I locked eyes with him, thinking of the first time Mash spoke that very word to me. Suddenly I exhaled a sigh of relief.

"That's it. You're doing great. Just stand there while I pretend I'm having the time of my life. And don't make any sudden moves like toss your hair to take away from the main characters shot." He explained.

"Now I have the urge to toss my hair."

"Don't do it." He grinned. "I would hate for you to get yelled at."

"So, what should I do?"

"Um, can you do a fake laugh? Better yet tell me about yourself." He placed his hand on his chin.

"What do you want to know?"

"How long have you been a P.A.? That is what you do, right?"

"No. I wrote this piece."

"Seriously. You're the writer? I thought you were Yogi's personal assistant."

"No. Just the boring writer. Yohan is teaching me the ropes. This is my debut."

"Congrats, and I don't find you boring at all. I just realized you don't have an accent."

"I'm from the states. North Carolina."

"New *Jers* born and bred, but I live in between L.A. and N.Y. now. How did you end up all the way over here?"

"Cut!" Yohan yelled.

"Don't move." Chili warned. "He may retake the scene, and you'll need to be in that exact spot...You were about to tell me how a writer from North Carolina ended up in England?"

"Love." I smiled.

"Love of the city?"

"No." I shook my head.

"I see. It must be love if you moved this far for him. I hope he doesn't mind me saying he has great taste."

"I don't mind you saying it. He knows what he has. And thank you." I placed my hand across my chest.

"Something tells me you get compliments all the time."

"Not all the time. Men say things, but aren't genuine."

Yohan called out to the room. "Places everyone. Roll 'em!"

Chili erased the look on his face from our conversation and returned back into his character. I stood still once again while he reenacted the same emotions as before for the camera.

"So, you do know what you're talking about," I said.

He flashed the top row of his teeth. "I've been doing this for a while. As you were saying."

I looked him in the eyes. "Men are unpredictable creatures. They say anything to get what they want and do whatever they please. So, when a man tells me I'm pretty, I say thank you. But I don't think they really mean it. They just see me as something they'd like to— you know, and then move on. You'd be surprised how many women suffer from self-esteem issues because of a man."

"Does this man of yours compliment you often?" Chili smoothed the baby hairs across his top lip.

"All the time. And he married me so…"

He smirked at my response and stared into my eyes. I knew then he was probing and sizing me up. I had to give it to him though. He was crafty.

"Ah, so you're off the market." He licked his lips. "Smart man. When you get a good one you better not let it slip through your fingers. Myself…I…ugh travel too much to settle down right now."

"Monogamy is hell for most men. The majority of them are bone collectors." I scoffed.

"Ouch. You did write this piece. Don't get me wrong, I want to settle down one day, but not any time soon. And she'd have to be the right woman."

"I hate when men say that— The right woman. As if women don't want the right man. We were all the right woman at some point, until some jerk came along and toyed with our emotions. I think men get high on pulling women's strings. You know what, my bad. I didn't mean to unleash my male bashing theories on you."

"It's cool. We're just vibing. And I got you to stop shaking on camera."

He was right. I got lost in our conversation and forgot the cameras were rolling. *Oh, he is good*. "Thank you for that. I'm totally not nervous anymore." I lowered my head and blushed. "Humor me. Why do men say they love…"?

"Cut! Okay we've got it!" Yohan shouted.

"What were you about to ask me?" Chili pulled on my blouse.

"It was nothing. Nice chatting with you. And thanks again."

I walked towards Olive arriving late on set.

She side-eyed me and spoke under her breath. "You looked like you were enjoying yourself over there."

We snickered.

"Yeah, watch out for him. He's a smooth one," I said.

"I sent you the invite for my brunch, but haven't received an rsvp. Are you and your better half going to be able to make it? The elderflower will be flowing."

"We'll be there. I had to check his schedule before I sent you a reply. Now you and your better half have a good night. I can't hang tonight."

On the drive home I caught myself smiling at Chili's flirtation, picturing Grams applauding in my head. "Have a backup plan," she said, but I wasn't that kind of woman, and Chili wasn't the type to become entangled with. He had nothing to lose, whereas I had everything to fumble. And just like that, I stopped toying with the idea of him as a play thing. I went home and led Mash to our bedroom where he pounded any thought of Chili from my mind, and realized the long hours, loneliness, and hurt burning inside of me was creating a fire I needed to put out.

ALL THE WAY UP

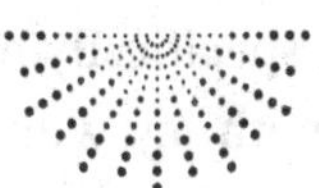

With careful maintenance, I had the best of both worlds—Interesting debates with Chili at work, and the delight of meaningful conversations with Mash at home.

In the meantime, ground was broken on the lot of our new home, while the sale of our current home in Virginia Water brought on anxiety. Stranger after stranger in and out of the house, violating our privacy with no follow-up, or offers to buy became unsettling. I loathed the outsiders walking through our personal space, touching our things, and seeing how we lived, so we moved into a flat in the city, leaving select pieces of furniture behind to be included in the sale.

Living out of suitcases, and being trapped between boxes and furniture tested our relationship. The temporary space was intimate, surrounded by everything imaginable from grocers, coffee shops, fitness classes, and the biggest change—

noise. Despite the latter, I enjoyed our new place. The ease and access of everything from shows, work, and shops had its appeal. It didn't beat living in the peaceful countryside, but the change was fresh and more importantly, necessary for our sanity and privacy.

The sanity part didn't last very long with the stress of designing a dream home. In terms of style, I wanted a mixture of the old world and the new. A classic exterior resembling historic England with a modern interior, and my personal lavatory. Mash loved the idea, but opposed one detail in the setup of my draft, causing strain between us.

"I maintain organization of my things better in the bathroom. Your side isn't as neat." I explained.

"Even as a single man, I specifically built a double vanity for the day I would share my life with my wife." He argued. "I like getting ready for bed together. You putting that goop on your face while I'm shaving. Me watching you primp to get ready. You want to take away something I couldn't wait to have."

Hearing his explanation filled me with guilt, but not enough to cave in with what I wanted.

I squeezed his lips. "That's very sweet, but I still want my own shower and vanity space. I don't like watching you brush your teeth, or being watched brushing mine. How could you have not picked up on that? Hell, I don't like watching people on TV brush their teeth. I'd also love it if I didn't sit in piss in the middle of the night, but fine, scrap my little piece of heaven from the plans."

"Do we at least agree on four bedrooms, a studio, a man cave, and an office?" He turned his head away from me.

I stared at him seething to himself. "And a pool."

He walked away flashing the 'Okay' symbol with his fingers.

I spazzed under my breath. "So, this is why couples bicker over building a house."

Mash stepped back into the bedroom. "What was that?"

"Nothing." I grinned.

Our disagreement suddenly made coming home the pit of my day, and going into work the peak. Having no space to find alone time forced us to deal with each other. And as time carried on without extra rooms to hide in, I realized I had changed. *Look at me being spoiled as if I hadn't lived most of my life in a starter home.*

Reshoots and overtime solved some of our problems, giving me a reason to come home just in time for dinner, after dinner, or near bedtime. And on the days we finished early and on time, I spent it hanging out with the cast and crew after work.

Mingling amongst them eased the sorrow I hid of feuding with my friends, and walking on eggshells in the flat. Serving the balance I needed as loneliness blossomed like a flower in the spring in my bones.

With my friends list shrinking, the weekend of Olive's brunch arrived right on time. I assumed her circle of cronies would be dressed in designer rags, and judge me from the texture of my hair to the nail polish on my toes. *Olive did call them bitches after all.* So, I made sure I was properly prepped, putting the husband's wallet to use.

We swung by the lot of our future residence on the way to Yohan's house. The progress was on target, if not further advanced. "We could be in here sooner by the looks of it." Mash clapped, smiling the blueprint was coming to life. "We did this." He emphasized. "You and I. Together."

"Yeah, I guess we did."

"I can't wait for us to move in. You have a surprise waiting for you inside. A few more weeks, we'll be christening every room."

A text in all caps from Khai popped up on my phone before I could respond. I muted my ringtone, and pulled Mash towards the car. "Come on. We're going to be late."

"Everything okay?"

"Yeah." I lied, covering my phone screen.

We left our future love nest, arriving on The Stallworth property minutes down the road.

Mash turned off the car. "It might be important. Go ahead and take it. You can't avoid them forever. I'll meet you inside."

I stood on the porch and braced myself for belligerence as I dialed Khai's number.

She answered. "Why haven't I heard from you?"

"I've been super busy. Is everyone alright?"

"You tell us." Shannon interrupted in the background. "That's right. She got you on speaker. I hear you have a new best friend. Are you liking your replacement?"

"Well, I can see where this conversation is headed, and since I'm at an event my new friend is hosting right now, I'll call you back."

"So, it's like that? Wow." Shannon fumed.

"We need to get together. Soon." Khai demanded.

"We can discuss that when I'm done here. I promise, I'll call you back."

I took a deep breath and regrouped before walking inside the chic, monochrome decorated weekend home of The Stallworths. It was beautiful. I suddenly understood why Olive said she would stay if he cheated. The perks, the homes, and the misery came as a package deal.

His house manager escorted me to the garden of paradise Olive called the sanctuary. The guests were assembled outside, separated by the sexes— The men gathered near the bar, and the women grouped by the courtyard's fire pit. I strolled towards Olive and her friends, suddenly taken aback at my name being shouted across the lawn.

"Nadia! Bring your cool ass over here! I was telling these guys about your man bashing theory! Come so I can prove you wrong!"

I froze in my steps and my shoulders tensed. Olive and I share a look of mortification, then I turned around on my toes to face the bar. "What in the hell is his problem?" I said under my breath. Mash's chest appeared still, and his face stern as a bull. A look I'd seen once in Copenhagen. My eyes roamed over to Yohan looking up at me behind his mug of beer, then over to Chili with an idiotic smile on his face.

In my mind the music came to a halt as I eased my path towards the group of gentlemen, praying the moment didn't lead to an altercation. I waltzed into Mash's arms and clamped my hands around his waist, then brilliantly improvised. "With everything going on in the world, you boys are over here talking about Venus versus Mars."

Mash placed his arm around my shoulder.

I asked him. "What have you been over here saying?"

"Just how lucky I am." He marked his territory with a kiss to my forehead.

"And you?" I turned to Chili. "Which one of my rants have you been over here getting twisted?"

"Hey, they were your words. Not mine. You know your theory about men really don't mean what they say when they complement a woman."

"I said men will say anything to get what they want, and do whatever they please. They don't mean half of the things they say to women." I corrected him.

"Now who wants to tell her she's wrong, besides me."

The men chuckled and sipped their beer until Yohan saved Chili from Mash's wrath. "Chili, you might want to quit while you're ahead. She has a point. Look at how many women we get with in a lifetime, and move on to the next. Can you honestly say you haven't said things you know a woman wants to hear, just so she will give you what you want?"

Chili stuttered. "We all have."

"Exactly my point. Men say whatever they need to get what they want. Case closed. Venus-1/Mars-0. Gentlemen, it was a pleasure. Now, don't sit over here and put nonsense into my husband's head. He's perfect the way he is." I tugged at his waist.

"Was everything alright with Khai?" Mash leaned in for a kiss.

I nodded yes.

Yohan chimed in. "How are your friends? Did they enjoy our presentation in Paris?"

Mash pinched my back and grinned.

I laughed internally. "Everyone is good. They enjoyed themselves and told me to thank you. It slipped my mind." My voice see-sawed. "Nice talking with you gentlemen."

I walked off looking back at Mash playfully, and toned down my strut towards the ladies, snickering to myself at Yohan's slick inquiry about Shannon. Olive and I locked eyes before I reached her. She lolled her head to the side and bellowed when I sat next to her near the fire.

"What the hell was he thinking?" She called for the waiter to serve me a glass.

"I wish I knew. Surely, he knew Mash was my husband. Right?" I scowled and rolled my eyes.

"Your days at the pub are done." Olive joked.

"You are probably right. Why are you and Yohan looking for a new house when you have this magnificent place? The landscape and the privacy are beyond breathtaking."

"He lived here with his ex-wife." Olive finished off her cocktail, then wiped the side of her mouth with her napkin.

"Say no more. I totally get it. I had to get used to the fact Mash has more than likely slayed a bitch, or two, or three in our house. I was so happy when he suggested we sell it and move."

"You understand me then."

I nodded. "So, who's who?"

She introduced me to her friends, Bianca and Nicola, and the wives of the men I'd just spoken with at the bar. They were all surprisingly welcoming and warm. I assumed they would be cold, and snooty like Olive on our first meeting.

After exchanging brief histories and discussing the way I pronounced certain words with my southern accent, we were seated to a table covered with teal linens and fuchsia florals. Olive arranged a seating chart, placing us at the table by name cards in front of shiny white dinner plates and sterling silverware.

Mash squeezed my thighs under the table, and I was less than inconspicuous with my reaction. The eyes of everyone in attendance were upon us until we settled down.

I complimented our hostess. "Olive this table setting is absolutely stunning."

Her brown cheeks turned rosy. "I can't take credit for it, but then again I will. Thank you, Nadia. I merely suggested the colors, and my party planner made the setting come to life."

A staff of hired hands entered the lawn every ten minutes with trays of soups, salads, vegan cuisine, and appetizers until the main course was served. Thirty minutes of boring business talk, taste tasting, and idle chatter ended with a smorgasbord of desserts to tide us over.

The conversation after dinner shifted to a unilateral discussion amongst everyone. Couples shared stories of how they met, creating a game of whose meet cute was the best. I sat quietly while Mash told our story, admiring his memory of small details from our beginning. The candlelight reflection in his brown eyes, and the way his lips curled when he said, "I knew she was the one when I let the track play all the way through," stirred me. We both blushed, recalling our kiss in the lobby the night before going to Glastonbury, and my insides tingled thinking about our trip to Ibiza. I never wanted him more in that moment, which was insane because I wanted him all the time.

I played with the hairs in his beard when he was done telling our meet cute story, and when he looked into my eyes I announced, "On that note we must say goodnight. Yohan and Olive, this was a magical evening and we thank you for inviting us into your home. It was lovely meeting you all and we must do this again."

We left the party and returned to our lot down the road, christening the Richmond air beneath the stars. I purred in Mash's ears as he rocked me sensuously in the backseat, feeling a connection of our souls travel between our bodies. Whatever the indescribable feeling was had to be love, because it was stronger than passion, and reminiscent of the morning I watched my friends leave me behind.

Weak from exertion, we opened the moonroof on the truck and stared at the stars in the sky, poking fun at our exit, and laughing at Yohan's obvious concern about Shannon.

"It kind of pissed me off." I confessed. "I mean Olive was only a few feet away. Men, I tell ya. Will one woman ever be enough?"

"I don't like the Chili fella. He's a prick and he likes you."

"He does not. He just thinks I'm cool because I speak my mind is all."

"I wanted to knock him on his ass when he shouted your name. It was embarrassing, and he acted too familiar with you. He had no idea I was your husband."

"Of course, he did. We've talked about you." I snuggled closer into him.

"What are you doing talking about me with him?" Mash scowled.

"Nothing personal like that. I'm just always saying my husband this and my husband that."

Mash huffed. "I don't like him."

"Point made. Tonight, was nice though, right?" My voice rose.

"The last fifteen minutes were." He kissed my head.

* * *

ON SET MONDAY MORNING, I raved about the soiree to Yohan. We shared a laugh at the highs and lows of the evening, Chili in particular, then he spoke candidly with me about my personal matter.

"I spoke with Shannon." He cleared his throat. "I wasn't sure I believed you when you said everything was okay. She told me you two are in the middle of a rift."

"It'll blow over I'm sure. My issue isn't with her anyways."

"She sent you a message. Or a joke. I'm not quite sure. Something about she'd be blue by now waiting for your call."

I chuckled.

"So, it was a joke I presume." Han glanced over his shoulder. "This poor fella." He kissed his teeth. "The young lad was quiet as a mouse after Mash cut him down like a tree with his eyes."

We snickered.

"Talk about embarrassing moments. For him and for me." I scrunched my face.

Yohan shook his head side to side.

Chili interrupted our conversation. "I hope I'm not interrupting anything. I just wanted to come over, and thank you for inviting me on Saturday. And Nadia, I realize I shouldn't have put you on the spot like that. I meant no harm."

His apology was overshadowed as the handsy man from the party in France fast approached our circle.

My stomach turned. "Everything's fine. My husband is cool." I lied to avoid reliving the moment.

The man from the party cleared his throat. "May I have a word with you?"

"Me?" I raised a brow.

"In private please. I'd prefer if we didn't speak family business in front of strangers. Besides, I don't think my son would like this one smiling in your face so much." He pointed to Chili.

Yohan brushed Chili on the shoulder. "Come on son." Then he turned to the strange man and shook his hand. "Senior, I didn't know you were dropping by today. Good seeing you. Have a word with me when you're done with your business here."

The stranger named Senior nodded. "Certainly,"

The familiarity in his voice shook me. With bright eyes I studied his features and knew when he said son, he meant Mash. He smiled in my face, and observed me from head to toe.

"Son?" I questioned him.

"Let me guess. He said I was dead. He thinks he can say it and make it true. That boy still has his mother's temper."

My heart fell to my knees.

"As you can see I'm alive and well. He's killed me off for far too long. I need you to get word to him for me. Tell him I've been unsuccessful in reaching him, and it's time we meet."

I stepped back. "I will not get involved in whatever it is going on between you two. Now if you'll excuse me."

Senior grabbed my arm. "Please do. And congratulate him on his upgrade."

I shrugged away from his grip. "That's the second time you've put your hands on me. I'm starting to get the impression you do whatever you like— Even when it's inappropriate."

"My dear, I was testing you and you passed. Maximus has selected well. And went all the way exotic this time. Tell him I approve and we need to speak. Lovely to meet you my dear."

I found my way to my chair and stared off into space while Yohan and Senior discussed their business near the exit. As I stewed over the now exposed lie Mash fed me over the years, I got lost in my own head. *'Why',* I wondered, replaying our conversation on the plane with Mr. Hunt over and over, remembering how Mr. Hunt raised his eyebrows when Mash said his dad was no longer with us. *'Why would he lie about such a thing, and why was his father not bothered by it?'*

This bombshell put another scratch on our record, and feelings of being naïve, stupid, and gullible resurfaced. I wondered, *'If he was lying to me about something as sensitive as family, what else could he be lying about?'* Then, Nomi was the first image to pop into my head. Sure he provided me with footage of the one night I questioned, but then I went down a rabbit hole and wondered how many other nights should I look into?

I was too upset to stay on set. I lied and told Yohan I wasn't feeling well, and headed home hoping Mash would be there. When he wasn't, I kicked a few boxes around and made my way to the couch, opened my favorite bottle of red, and silenced my phone.

Drinking straight from the bottle, I fumed, formed scenarios in my head of Mash living the Rockstar life when I didn't accompany him on trips, and I placed him in the same category as the asshole who stained me with insecurities, and doubt. Dylan.

The light from my messages caught my attention. I clicked on the email icon, and opened up a message with Paid Writing Opportunity in the subject line, forwarded to me from Chili.

"Before I was rudely insulted and ran off earlier, I was going to mention a

buddy of mine has this opening back home. I hope you submit. Hope you're feeling better and see you on set."

I drank to that and passed out on the sofa. Mash arrived home hours later, hammered and hot-headed.

He nudged my feet and woke me. "Nads."

I looked up and smart-mouthed him. "You found friendship with the bottle tonight, too."

"I had a few with Prano at the pub. I've been calling you for hours. What gives?" He stood over me with his hands tucked inside the pouch of his hoodie.

I sprung to my feet and stood in his face. "What gives is I met my father-in-law today. The father you claimed died. The mystery man who put his arm around me was your father. I think you knew that all along, and kept it from me. He sent a message. He wants to see you."

Mash tugged on my hip. "Let me explain."

I held up my hand to silence him. "He also said to tell you he approves, and you went all the way exotic this time. He's a real charmer that one."

"He said what!"

"Should I have been offended, or flattered?"

"Nadia, he's dead to me. Don't ever call him your father-in-law again. Am I clear? Stay away from him."

"How? He's a financial backer of my project."

"Listen. My... That man is not someone you want to get entangled with."

"Why would you lie to me about him?" I rose from the sofa.

"He's tied in scandal. He's untrustworthy. He's selfish and manipulates everything. It's his way or no way."

"I can see the father-son resemblance there." I stormed off.

"Don't..." He reached for me.

"Don't what? Point out the obvious control freak tendencies you share? For fucks sake, what did he do to make you lie about him being dead?"

"He slept with Nomi!"

Mash paced the floor and ran his fingers through his hair, then down his face over and over.

The rage in my eyes burned. "Ugh! I knew I wasn't done hearing that bitch's name!" I squeezed through the boxes, made my way into the bedroom, and locked the door.

Mash pressed against it. "You wanted to know why! Well there you have it! She is the reason I don't have a relationship with my father!"

I kept silent. So, did he. His footsteps rescinded down the hall then returned. The door suddenly opened, and he stood between the panels with a butter knife in his hand.

I rolled my eyes at him. "That is reason enough we have to get out of here." I pointed to the knife.

He sat next to me on the bed. "He always looked at her with lust in his eyes, then would preach to me "Son, she isn't worthy of our name. She's an opportunist.""

"You can spare me the details."

"Then I saw them having dinner in the city. I watched every move he made on her, how she responded, and how she went to his high rise with ease. They had no idea I was onto them, and I caught her in his bed. My father looked at me guiltless. "I told you son." Is all he said, and that was the last time I saw him."

I felt bad for him. He experienced something similar if not worse than I had with Taylor and Dumbass, but my anger and annoyance wouldn't allow me to comfort him.

I spoke without compassion. "That's a sad story, but I simply don't care. I'm sick of this woman being a part of my life. Our life. She has too much power over you. You've allowed her to disrupt us twice now, and ruined your relationship with your father. Is she the one that got away?" My eyes turned glossy.

"The one?" He scoffed. "How can you say this to me? I've done nothing but show you, you are the one. What else do I have to do to make you see how much you mean to me?" He held my feet in his hands.

"Sometimes I feel like I'm dreaming. Like this isn't real. It's too perfect at times, so I wait for something to go wrong, like this, to remind me nothing is perfect."

"Nadia, nothing's perfect. I'm not. Not even you."

"What other shocking revelation is out there waiting to punch me in the face? Do you have any children I need to know about? Tell me now if you do."

"I'm not hiding any secrets from you."

I teared up. "I think a part of you still loves her."

Mash's face turned red. He withdrew his hand and rose from the bed. "You're talking insane right now. I'm over her. I'm over my mother's sperm donor. And I'm over this conversation." He stormed out of the room.

I followed him screaming. "You don't get to turn this off because you're embarrassed! You know why! Because you lied! She was your girlfriend and you told me she was just a fuck buddy! And I think you still love her and don't want to admit it! But guess what! I forgive you for being stupid, and for falling in love with a dope-head heaux who was fucking you, your daddy and your friends!"

Mash walked out on me. He picked up his keys, slammed the door, and left without saying a word. It was our worst fight to date, but I was okay with him being gone. Him spending a few days at the old house gave me time to sulk, scream, and submit to every project I came across to deal with the shift in our relationship. Unfortunately, time and space didn't heal what was broken between us.

17

WELCOME TO THE JUNGLE

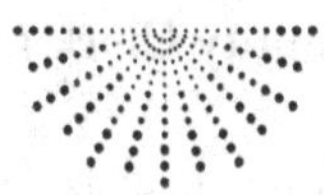

The couple of days we spent apart were damaging. My words went too far and bruised his ego. I hurt his feelings, though he would never admit it. We were back to where we were months ago when he threatened my behavior needed to change, except this time we both were having tantrums.

When he returned to our apartment, I was happy to see him walk through the door, but I didn't smile like usual at the sight of him. My love wasn't stronger than my pride when it should have been, and he was now giving me a taste of my own medicine. The silent treatment.

Two adults living on top of each other in a tiny flat, waiting for the other to crack became unbearable. I could have taken his return as an apology, but I needed to hear the words, even though hearing *I'm sorry* didn't really justify the lie he told.

Eventually I'd forgive him, but the analytic side of me couldn't let it go. The naïve side of me believed him when he said he no longer loved Nomi, but still I slipped into a place of desolation and imagination— Thinking the worst, because I was used to it. I wanted to hurt him before he hurt me, which would solve nothing, yet I couldn't resist the urge to strike the first blow.

A week of no communication turned into weeks of avoiding one another. Our newly built house was near completion and gave us a reason to talk, but the excitement disappeared, and I couldn't muster the courage to tell him I wasn't moving in it with him.

The torment of our disagreement led me to ask Yohan for a favor. After being passed over on the project Chili recommended, Han pulled a few strings with one of his friends in New York, landing me a gig as a Continuity Clerk for ninety days. Therein lied the first blow.

Even though we weren't talking, Mash was livid I would be away for three months, and demanded I decline the opportunity.

"How selfish can you be? The house is ready for us to move in." He fussed.

"I applied since we aren't getting along. You should move in. You hate this flat anyway."

"You're doing it again. All you know how to do is run." He exhaled deeply against one of the boxes in the living room.

I loved him. Missed him even, but something was off between us, and I couldn't move into that house feeling disconnected from him. He was also right. Running was what I did best and who I was.

"I can't move in that house with this bad energy between us. Hopefully we can work on us when I get back." I slipped past him.

He pulled me close and kissed me. "Turn it down for us."

This was the Maximus Sharper I knew. The man who'd been missing the past few weeks. I looked into his mesmerizing eyes and wondered where he'd wandered off to, and kissed him back.

"Where have you been?" I tapped his chest.

He leaned his forehead against mine and squeezed me tight. His pants tightened at the zipper causing my slit to pulse. I wanted to feel him fuck the frustration between us away, but refrained this time, knowing our problem would still exist after the pleasure of us bumping pelvises subsided.

"You always get your way. Not this time," I said. "I leave in the morning."

When I woke, Mash was asleep next to me in the bed. I expected him to play on my weakness for him. Looking at me with sad doughy eyes, and trailing me from room to room while I packed. He hit me with those four letters that made my heart flutter. "Stay," he said, when the taxi blew his horn.

Tempted and weak, my knees locked and my fingers trembled. With my back turned to him I paused in the threshold of the door. The leather from the carry-on slipped from my grip then I caught it. I turned around and stepped into my teary-eyed husband, kissed him passionately on his lips and whispered in his mouth. "I'll call you when I land."

Thousands of feet high above the Atlantic, I smiled at my reflection against the backdrop of the clouds. I no longer felt like the naïve, needy girl controlled by feelings and love, but a woman taking charge of her destiny and dreams.

As promised, I called home when I landed. Mash didn't pick up. The town car Yohan reserved for my arrival delivered me to the upper eastside of Manhattan to Olive's apartment.

Luxurious and very much to her taste, I felt uncomfortable living in her upscale pad. The layout was *decked* for a Grecian Goddess with gold fixtures and installed lamps on the walls covered with linen wallpaper, black speckled marble floors, and furniture that no one ever brushed against their cheeks.

I feared being accused if something went missing, or leaving a print on the beige sofa, a stain on the wooden coffee table, or a chip on the good china. Then, I entered the bedroom and knew I didn't belong. It was color coordinated in hues of grays and teal to perfection. The walls were covered with suede, and as I ran my fingers across a foot of the fabric, my handprint left its trace and I finalized my decision. I could not stay there. It was dust free due to the weekly maid service, and had a spacious kitchen I was sure Olive never set foot in, but not even the twenty-four-hour security, and doorman could bring me peace in her quarters.

I tossed and turned all night on the silk sheets, sliding to the edge and wrapped up with a pillow as the sounds of the neighbors, and creaks in the walls kept me awake. I checked my phone throughout the night, crying silently over the distance between my better half who still hadn't returned my call. No text, no missed messages, no communication whatsoever, and it felt like the beginning of the end for us.

I beat the sun, rising early to fix breakfast, cleaned behind myself, and questioned the doorman on availability in the building. Shortly after the leasing office opened, I signed a month to month lease for my own studio apartment, one floor above Olive's. It was smaller, cheaper, and empty, but it was mine. And inside my very own walls, I cried my eyes out on borrowed sheets from Olive's apartment on an inflated mattress in the middle of the living room floor.

At 5 a.m., the ringtone for Mash woke me. *"Day three seems promising,"* I thought, answering his call and exposing my puffy eyes and anguished face. We looked at each other through our screens and said nothing for more than half a minute.

Then, I broke the silence. "What is it? My appearance? Or are you still pissed I left?"

"I'm sorry."

"For what?" I rolled over and propped my phone against the pillow.

"Everything. My words, my lack thereof, my not seeing you off. The way I've treated you these past few weeks. Just everything." He dropped his head. "How are you?"

I sighed. "Fine I guess. As you can see I need to give myself a facial, and do something about de-puffing my eyes."

"You look beautiful from where I'm sitting." He grinned.

"And you're lying to me again."

"Nadia. I didn't call to argue. We've done enough of that for a lifetime in my opinion. There's ninety days between us. We shouldn't have let it begin like this."

"I agree. But I think we'll manage. We have before."

"Not for this long, but hopefully it'll go by quick. You know I love you. Right?"

"I know."

Leaving London was meant to hurt him, but I hurt myself in the process. Looking at his glum face, I knew I delivered a mighty blow. And him looking at mine, told him I regretted my hasty decision. But this was one of many storms we had to weather, and right now I needed him to be wet for a while.

I perked up a bit after hearing Mash's voice. I got dressed to do some home shopping, and walked a few blocks, familiarizing myself with the neighborhood. I stopped at the first hardware store on my route. Quickly, I learned I was on home soil, but not in the south. The clerk was overly direct, not too friendly, and never smiled when he made eye contact with me. He asked how he could help me, took my key from my hand, scorched my ears with his machine, and passed my set of keys to me.

While paying him I asked, "Is there a post office near here?"

He took my money and passed me my change. "One block up." Then carried on as if I wasn't still standing there.

The exchange left me staggered. I collected my feelings, used a search engine to find the post office, and stood in line to mail the extra key to Mash. A few of the customers hissed at me for not having my order together as I stood at the desk filling out the envelope. I rushed to sign my note and kissed it with my plum lips. As I passed the line on my way out, an elderly woman said, "He better be worth holding up the line honey."

I was culture shocked, having gone from the south where everyone says hello, to grand London where everyone judges you, now to New York where no one seemed to give a fuck. I often felt I didn't belong amongst the Europeans with my southern charm. Oddly enough, I felt the same in New York.

I wanted to race back to my apartment and hide, but I still needed to go shopping. I taxied about to a furniture store, ordered a bed and a sofa, and finished my day buying drapes and rods, pots and pans, kitchen utensils and one necessary wine glass for my short stay.

The city was loud, fast paced, and crowded. So was London, but this was a different type of crowded. It was fashionable, but not as posh as the places I'd seen during my short time living abroad, and less regal in a way.

The location of the studio wasn't in the safest area of the city, and with the long, late hours we worked, I racked up a plethora of taxi charges. One time riding the pissed-fumed subway was enough of the New York experience for me. Of all my grievances, it was the worst of them all with one good take away. I saw a woman sitting alone, dressed provocatively, but happy. She glowed in her seat, her fishnet stockings with random holes covered her crossed legs swinging her combat boots freely. Her flat stomach exposed by a cutoff baseball crop top, and flamingo pink hair cut low on one side. She smiled to herself, nodding to whatever pleased her ears through her ear pods, and I couldn't help but watch in wonder what her happiness looked like on the inside. Her smile was so infectious it made me smile from looking at her, and she winked at me before she swung through the open doors. I smiled even bigger from her notion, taking the exchange with me at the next stop.

Within a week, the train became the only thing I didn't fancy. I quickly adapted to the snaps, brisk tongues, quick wit, fast pace, crowded streets, loud fashion, colorful city of go getters. If I had followed my dreams and moved here when I graduated high school, I would be exactly like the city folk I feared. Remembering that made me fall in love with The City of Dreams in a New York minute.

The loneliness balanced itself with fatigue of working long hours. I missed the comfort of Mash lying next to me. How I slid my feet under his leg, and the warmth of his body behind me. To make up for his absence, I found a general store and purchased a heated blanket. Between that and the sound of waves on my computer, I slept like a baby high above the noise outside.

Flowers began appearing at my door every morning, bonding my only friendship in town with the doorman. He pitied me for my lack of a social life, which changed my third week in the city.

Chili came to town for an audition, and invited me to join him and some friends at a bar one Friday night. I jumped at the chance to be amongst people, familiar or not, and experience my first taste of the city that never sleeps.

On my way home from work, I took note of a massive street ad, and copied the look from the model. I dressed my fitted A-line skirt with a pair of sleek boots, a plain long-sleeved black tee, and a geo-printed belt with a wide buckle to tie in the two pieces. I dressed up the tee with a chunky brass necklace, and layered my wrists with brass and oatmeal bracelets, topping everything off with a form-fitting wrap trench.

The first to arrive of my party, I waited at the bar, and ordered a fuzzy navel to play it safe. The bartender and the gentleman sitting closest to me laughed at my drink of choice.

"Where are you from?" the bartender asked.

I knew he detected I wasn't from the city. "Long story," I replied.

"Tell you what. I'll make you a real drink, on the house."

"As long as it's not too strong, I'll try it." I flipped my shoulders to remove my coat.

Closely I watched him combine my peach schnapps with grenadine, vodka, pineapple juice, and either cranberry or cran-grape juice, and one other ingredient in a titanium mixing shaker. He poured it in a tall glass and topped it with a cherry, then presented me with his creation.

"Cheers. Welcome to the city newbie." He smiled.

The patron who laughed at my choice tilted his head slightly to watch me sip on the concoction. I swallowed a good bit, and raised my eyebrows as the flavors came to life in my mouth.

"Damn this is good. Thank you." I lifted the glass to salute him.

"A bartender loves customer praises." He smirked, wiping a glass dry with a cloth.

"I think you just made a new customer, Al. She looks like she'll be back for another one of whatever you mixed up," said the guy sitting closest to me.

"I hope so." Al winked.

"Al, my new friend, you should market this."

"I just mix the drinks, not copyright them." He teased.

"So, was Al right? Are you a newbie, because you look fresh to me?" said the guy next to me.

He adjusted his black and gray scarf which matched the hairs on his beard, and removed his navy-blue wool coat from his broad shoulders.

"You don't look like most of the women around here. Your aura is fresh." He added.

"Like I said, long story." I turned my head.

"I have time. I just got off of work and came down here to support my main man Al. Tell me your long story." He revealed one dimple on his caramel shaded face.

I pursed my lips and sipped. "My mother taught me not to talk to strangers."

He laughed. "We can change that."

Al watched our exchanged with a grin on his lips. I shook my head and sneered at the persistent gentleman.

"Can I get back to my drink now?"

He coughed. "Sure, if you'll let me buy you a second one."

"Is offering free drinks how you get what you want from women? Liquoring up the unsuspecting prize?"

"Not at all. I'm just trying to make a friend, but I think she is telling me to get lost the nicest way possible. I definitely know you aren't from around here. A New York girl wouldn't be as nice as you. She'd flat out tell me to fuck off."

"You're very perceptive."

"I am." He bragged.

"If your timing was right, I would tell you my name, where I'm from, and sit at this bar and be your friend all night, but I can't, so please accept my apologies."

"There's that nice girl again. I like you."

"You don't know me to like me."

"Right again, but I'd like to."

We stared at each other for a few seconds after his brilliant comeback. He tilted his head back and swallowed the shot Al placed in front of him, rubbed his robust chest, then looked at me and smiled.

"So friend." I interrupted him. "It's been a pleasure, but my party just arrived. Thanks for the conversation."

The guy looked over his shoulder at Chili, and lost the smile on his face. "Nice talking to you, too, lady whose name I didn't get."

Chili hugged me in a close, strange manner, and my face scowled. The guy at the bar noticed my expression and raised an eyebrow.

"You sure you know this guy?" he asked.

I nodded. "Yeah, Chili this is…ugh" I wound my hand in a circle.

"Lucas. Lucas Fleming." He ogled Chili.

"Chili Walker."

"I was just keeping the pretty lady here company. You two enjoy your evening." Lucas smirked at me.

"We will. I see you got started without me." Chili joked.

"Courtesy of my new friend, Al." I waved goodbye.

I followed Chili a few steps away to the booth his friends reserved. He introduced me to everyone, then ordered another round of drinks for the table. I asked our waitress to get the bartender to make his special drink for me, and raised my hand when she relayed the message. In turn, Lucas saluted me as if I was signaling him, and we shared a laugh together from afar.

Chili placed his arm above my seat. "Looks like you've made yourself a new friend."

I leaned away from him. "I wouldn't say friend. I never told him my name. But did you catch the pretty remark. I told you men use compliments all the time to run game on a woman."

Chili looked at me weird. "He wasn't lying though."

Bewildered by his remark, I turned to the stage as the band began playing a combination of new jazz fused with hip-hop and spoken word. I was no longer in Kansas anymore. After two years of being surrounded around techno mashups, and dancehall reggae, I found myself missing home, lost in the rhythmic sounds of Harlem.

The night turned out to be fun. I retired my bartender special after losing count of how many I had consumed, and recognized the dangerous look in Chili's eyes. His friends called it a night in the middle of the band's second set, and I followed their lead to make a clean getaway. Chili kept me trapped in the booth as they scurried off, gazing at me with that weird look again.

He slid close and I asked him. "Have you had one too many?"

Yelling over the music, he scooted closer to me. "Nadia, I've been meaning to ask if you like living out here?"

I remained facing the stage. "It's cool. And only temporary."

A purring sound rolled from between his teeth. "Temporary... Right. Are you eager to return to London?"

I took a deep breath and faced him. "Why the inquisition, Chili?"

Staring into my eyes, he smiled at me then angled his head forward. "If you ever find yourself in L.A. I have my own place. You could stay with me if and when you score a job out west. Unfortunately, when I come to New York, I stay with friends. If I had my own pad out here, I would have put you up."

"And I would have declined..."

He cut me off. "I dream about you sometimes. On an intimate level."

"And you're telling me this because?" I raised my eyebrows.

"Because I can't stop thinking about you. Your husband was crazy to let you come out here alone. I know I'm overstepping, but I'd be a fool not to shoot my shot."

"Chili you're cute and all, but I see you as a..."

"Don't say friend." He interrupted me again. "Kiss me and see if you still want to end your sentence the same way." He aimed for my face.

I curved him and pulled out my vibrating phone which read '911' from Khai.

"Who is Khai?" Chili inquired.

I pressed my phone against my chest, furrowed my brows, and sucked my teeth at him. "You have had one too many." I dialed Khai's number. "Hey, it's late and loud in here, what's the emergency?"

"I'm not supposed to tell you this, but Mash is in New York. Taylor overheard Levi talking to him. His flight just landed. I thought I would give you a heads up. You know since we are supposed to be friends, but you seem to have forgotten that." Khai sassed me.

"Thanks for telling me. I'll call you when..."

"Whenever you get the chance. I know." Her voice dragged. "Sounds like you're having a good time."

A sarcastic laugh escaped me. "We'll talk."

Khai hummed. "Um hmm. Good night."

Chili might as well have been on the call with me as close as he sat to eaves drop. I faced him to finish our awkward conversation. "Where was I?" I exhaled. "I was saying I see you as a good friend, but after tonight, I don't think we should speak for a while. And I lied to you before. My husband doesn't think you're cool. He detests you, actually."

I slid from the opposite end of the booth and skedaddled passed the bar to the exit. "Fuck," I mumbled at the traffic speeding by, preventing me from crossing the street to jump in an empty cab illegally parked.

I returned near the line of patrons waiting to get inside the club, ordered a car, and shivered for five minutes until the Lyft arrived. I hopped in and reached for my seatbelt when the back door on the other side opened.

"My man, can you credit her account and accept cash for this ride?" Lucas leapt in.

"No, I cannot," the driver answered.

"So where are we going?" His eyes stretched without blinking.

"I'm going home, and you are getting out."

"My man, drop me off two blocks ahead. Here is a fifty for your trouble." He handed the driver. "And here is a fifty for your ride home."

"I don't need your money." I smirked, pushing the bill forward towards him.

"If you don't take it, I'll tip my man right here." He smiled.

"Tip him."

Lucas dropped the fifty in the passenger seat. "My man that's for you."

The driver nodded.

Lucas looked over at me smiling wide, pleased with himself. The driver didn't fuss since he was paid off, and watched us from the rearview mirror.

"Hey guy, I don't know." I sat confused and flustered.

"Lucas."

"Look Lucas, I'm not impressed by your money."

"What is it about you? At least tell me your name?"

"If I tell you, will you leave me alone?"

"No."

At least he's honest.

"It's Nadia."

"Damn, that name fits you." He purred and closed his eyes. "Very sexy. I must admit when you walked away with that square at the bar I said to myself, *'She is a real woman. What could a clown like him possibly know what to do with a woman who is right under the hood?'* I saw him try to kiss you. Why'd you shoot him down?" Lucas chuckled.

"Because he's not my man."

"So, you have a man?" His eyes locked on me.

"I have a husband."

"Where is he?"

"Waiting for me to come home."

"Nah, you're bullshittin' me. He wouldn't let you come out and be with ole boy alone. Unless he doesn't know." Lucas gave me the side-eye.

"Ole boy is a co-worker, and my husband had to work so he couldn't join us tonight." I turned to the window, avoiding his eyes.

"I don't think "your husband" would approve of you having drinks with someone trying to kiss you, Nadia."

"Should I tell him?"

Lucas eye-fucked me for a few seconds and licked his lips. His fingers played with his chin hair as he pouted his mouth. "Nah. Save him the trouble."

I amused him. "If you were him, would you want to know?"

"Can't say." He shrugged. "I'd like to know you though."

"I belong to someone else is all you need to know about me."

"Why all the secrets?"

"It's complicated." I pressed my lips together.

"I'd like to hear about complicated." He stared at me until I smiled. "My man, right here is good."

Tapping on the back of the front seat, he broke his gaze, then gave me a once over. The driver pulled over to the side of the street, and Lucas reached inside his coat pocket.

"Ms., I mean Mrs. Nadia, here is my card. You see the sign above those lampposts? You can find me there. Second floor. Whenever you want to tell someone about your complication. Call me, or stop by. Either way I hope to see you again. Driver make sure she gets home safe. Good night."

Lucas jumped out of the car and tapped on the roof. The driver drove off looking at me in the rearview, leering at me as I threw the card in my bag. I pretended I didn't see him judging me, and hid my face from him as I smiled looking out of the window.

During the drive to my apartment, my mind raced about Mash's surprise visit. This opportunity was supposed to serve as a needed separation to self-examine, and heal from his lies. We needed to miss each other for a bit, and I was enjoying the courtship of flowers at my door, and messages of poetry, and song lyrics sent to my phone throughout the day. But then I opened the door of the car when it pulled in front of my building, and grew excited about his visit.

I raced upstairs and showered the club smell off of me, turned on my heating blanket, and threw on my pajamas. I read two chapters of a novel by the time I heard him outside of the door. I placed my bookmark between the pages and felt my nipples sharpen. "Is someone there?" I asked, loud enough for him to hear me. He turned the second lock and walked in, looking like Christmas morning. Before I could say what are you doing here, he rushed over and held me in his arms so tight I could barely breathe.

"I can't live without you," he said.

I clung to him, sniffing for his natural scent, and melting at the touch of his hands against my back. "What took you so long?"

"You took me so long. I tried to give you the space you wanted, but I had to see you. Then this key arrived, so I took it as an invitation. Did you really think I would let you spend your thirtieth birthday alone?"

"I told you, I'm not looking forward to it. It depresses me really."

"I still couldn't let my favorite girl bring in this big one alone. Babe, I may have fucked up and kept a huge secret from you, but it was for a good reason. I really hope these past few weeks has been enough time for you to forgive me."

"I have forgiven you." I pinched his chest.

"I see you haven't done much with the place." He took off his coat.

"This isn't home. Three months and I'm out." I snapped my fingers.

"What if you get more assignments here?"

"A bridge to cross later. Go shower so we can go to bed."

I waited for him under the sheets *pantyless*. He climbed in wearing a towel around his waist, and laughed at how warm the bed felt.

"Is this how you've replaced me?" He joked, feeling my prickled skin and kissing on my neck.

"It's cold here. Even colder without you to keep me warm at night…"

He shut me up with a kiss on the lips, wrapped his body around mine, and linked our fingers. "Sheesh your feet are freezing!" He jumped.

"You could rub them and warm them for me."

"I planned on rubbing something else."

His hands massaged my hips while we kissed looking into each other's eyes. He propped me on top of him and removed my shirt, fondling the curves of my breasts with a gentle brush of his fingers. Adoring me from below, he reached for my face and propped himself up with the strength of his abdomen to taste my mouth with a tender kiss, then gently bit my top lip.

I gyrated on his lap. "Somebody missed me," he said, fiddling in my wetness.

I opened the towel and traced the vein on his brick hard pipe with two fingers. "Somebody missed me."

Heat took over my body and I slid down his shaft, gasping from his girth, relaxed from his presence. I welcomed him and sat there taking it all in, carousing in the feels and remembering to breathe. The freshly spritzed cologne from his wrists ignited my senses as I sucked his fingertips, receiving all of him and the slow, hard pressed strokes he saved for me. Throttled and untamed tugs at my peak made my limbs shudder. My back went numb from the twitching of his head budding inside of me.

"Already." He grinned.

"It's been a while." I whimpered, gripping his bell-end between my legs.

"Allow me." He spun me on my back.

Submissively I ordered. "Do whatever you want with me."

I begged for a rough course of action than the gentle ride I gave him. But he ignored my command, and took his time with my pussy. Tending to my every need, my every inch, with plunges to remind my throbbing center who she belonged to.

My walls clung to his cock as sighs of relief released from my mouth, and the sides of my warm embrace curved to his delight. He felt just as I remembered. Maybe better. Distance did our bodies good, and Mr. Sharper came into town to fuck the nonsense out of me.

I listened to him whisper my name and confess his love. His craving for my folds brought out the passion we neglected. The desire we abandoned overflowed with me melting beneath him, capturing a moment to be remembered.

He was close when the perfected pounding paused in my pussy, and his hips thrust further into me. I grazed his shoulder with my teeth, and pulled his head back to see the look on his face when he could no longer hold it back. He hollered in delight, his elation read across his open mouth. I smiled to myself, proud to give him what he came for, and happy to receive the gift he carried below his belt.

He rolled me back on top of him and kissed my forehead, then my cheeks, then my neck, squeezing my thighs tightly against him to seep out his pearls.

"Can we do this all night?" he asked.

"I damn sure hope so."

18
WHEN CAN I SEE YOU

Our tanks were on empty by morning, but the courtship continued once we gained energy to roam the nearby streets for lunch. Inertly, we strolled hand in hand into a corner deli, ordering from every section of the menu, reminiscent of the many times we travelled abroad.

I choked on a sweet potato fry, completely won over as Mash asked me out on a date like he needed my permission. It was like a scene from an old movie, him pulling out two tickets from the inside pocket of his jacket to see a Broadway show. My cheeks beamed of flattery. Oh be still my beating heart. The planning he put into this visit made my body tingle, and I could feel myself falling for him all over again.

By nightfall we were witnessing Hollywood and New York legends work their magic on stage, followed by a late dinner in uptown. To finish the evening off, we strolled under the bright lights of Times Square with the other tourists.

In the midst of the hustle and bustle, I took Mash's hand. "Can we talk without arguing?"

His eyelids flinched. "What's on your mind?"

"Why didn't you want me to know Nomi was more than a friend?"

The tension in his hands tightened. "What did you think about me when we met?"

"I thought— damn he's fine…and I thought it was smooth how you sent for me…and I thought you had good energy."

"Now think back to my former management. Davie created the image of me as a "ladies' man" every woman desired. After hearing something over and over, you start to believe it. So here I am this "ladies' man", yet the one girl I thought I had a connection with sleeps with my father. Not a younger guy. Not another celebrity. The old man from which I came. What kind of ladies' man loses his girl to his father?"

"I get it's embarrassing, but trust me when I say it had nothing to do with you. When your dad said she wasn't worth your last name he proved it. She was a whore out for money."

"But I got played. If word got out, which is what she has been threatening to tell the media, my image would have been ruined. I'd be a laughing stock."

"Here's the headline. 'Heartthrob Loses Whore to Millionaire Father'." I grinned in his face.

"We know you're a writer. You don't have to show off."

"I'm trying to make you laugh. Lighten up. What they did to you is similar to what Taylor and my ex did to me. Betrayal is a bitch. I kind of know how you feel."

"You know they were the reason why I stopped getting high. Except for the bud." He explained. "I have nothing left for her, but my dad…I can't be a part of his life. Using the old I'm your dad and was trying to show you she was a gold-digger speech. I don't buy it."

"I say forgive him, but keep him at a distance."

Mash stopped moving his feet. "We're being kind here, so don't take offense to what I'm about to say. Stay out of it. Please. You don't know him."

"Then at least see what he wants."

"I'll think about it." He squeezed my hand. "Letting him in is like inviting the devil inside for tea."

"Well I'm from the south and we drink sweet tea."

He looked over at me and attempted to laugh, but something held him back. The worried look in his eyes told me to leave the conversation about his father right there on the street.

The ambiance of the city carried us into a risqué moment of passion, equivalent to a taxi-cab confession scenario, turning the driver's car into a make out mobile. "Please, no, not in here." The driver begged, watching our foreplay in his rearview mirror.

The mood for another wild fuck fest had been set. Mash tipped the cabbie generously for his trouble, then we ran inside my lease to finish each other off with a double play. For the first time in months, Sunday morning felt like a Sunday morning. I cooked breakfast, we lied in bed, watched a movie, did crossword puzzles, and napped until past noon.

"How is the house?" I asked him when I woke.

He turned to face me. "I wouldn't know."

"What do you mean?"

"I'm still in the flat. I'm not moving into the house until you come home." He caressed the side of my face. "I know when you left, you were telling me to fuck off."

"I would never." I smirked.

"I'll put a for sale sign up before I live in there without you."

"Tell me you've at least walked through it? Took pictures?"

"I did a walk through, and I have the keys, but the move in date is up to you."

"Mash, you hate living in the flat, and I'm going to be here for two more months."

He huffed and sat back on his pillow. I didn't have the heart to tell him he had to be rid of his demons before I would move in. We were getting along so well I changed the subject, and asked the other burning question on my mind.

"How long do I have you for?"

"Forever." He sighed.

"I meant when is your flight home?"

"I know what you meant. I leave on Wednesday. Are you tired of me already?"

"Actually, I don't want you to leave. We seem like us here."

He pulled me on his chest and kissed me on the lips. "I know what you mean. Feels like we've found our mojo again."

Before the city lost daylight, we took advice from one of his friends and checked out street performers on 42nd, then grabbed a pizza for dinner from a parlor two blocks away from my building.

I woke to an empty bed in the morning. A note rested under my arm with instructions to be dressed to impress by the time he returned. I played hooky for work, and dolled up like I was told.

Mash waltzed through the door holding a huge chocolate cupcake with a single candle stuck in the center, alongside a box of cronuts.

"It's not much, but I remember you saying you wanted to try these." He revealed the goodies.

"You remembered." I hummed.

"I pay attention. You have to place an order weeks in advance for these things. You should have seen the line. It was wrapped around the block. Happy birthday baby. Welcome to the thirties." He closed in and planted the sweetest kiss on my lips. "I love you. You want to open the cronuts first?"

I professed my love in return, and tore open the breakfast box full of sugary blend of donuts and croissants rolled into one. It was the perfect beginning to my day, followed by a morning full of laughs.

Then, he revealed my next surprise. A hired photographer curated a photo session of us in Central Park, prior to Mash shuttling me off to FAO Schwartz.

"You said you wanted that floor piano. When you're done jumping up and down on it, I hope you jump and down on me." He gently bit my cheek.

"You remembered that?" I gazed in his shiny, brown eyes. "You've thought of everything." My head rest on his chest.

"You'll get how much I love you one day."

For the next thirty-six hours, I nestled in his arms, ordered take out, and breathed the same air, consumed with the stench of one another, mixed aromas of food, and soiled sheets.

I cried when we said goodbye Wednesday evening. My feelings about my decision slightly changed about applying for the assignment now that we were back on good terms, but the little voice inside my head told me we needed the distance to get the resolve I was hoping for—for him to be free of the hold his ex had over him, and to mend his relationship with his father so we could move forward.

After spending a long weekend locked inside, I was happy to return to work and learn something new. The faster we completed the assignment, the faster I could return to London, and end my lonely nights in the city that never sleeps.

The week went by slow now that Mash was gone, and by the weekend, the loneliness and boredom crept back in. Monday morning, I volunteered to help setup for a seminar at NYU with the idea of keeping myself busy would help the time go by faster.

When the panel broke off for the day, I toured the campus, travelling down the road of what could have been my life if granted another choice. As I walked the grounds, I stumbled upon the library filled with undergrads.

An unattended phone at the check-in desk called to me. I convinced myself to make the most of the day when Lucas crossed my mind. I dug inside my purse and rolled the dice. The devil on my shoulder wanted him to keep me company. The angel on my other shoulder prayed he didn't answer.

"Lucas Fleming speaking."

"Damn," I mumbled.

"This is Lucas Fleming."

"Hey, I um. I wasn't expecting you to answer. It's the weekend. Figured you'd be busy, and not at work."

"Who is this?" he asked.

"I shouldn't have called. Sorry to bother you."

"Nadia, I'm playing with you. I recognize the accent. I'm surprised to hear from you."

"I'm surprised I called." I grew hot with guilt.

"The line says NYU?"

"Yeah, I on the campus wrapping up work, but I'm about to leave so."

"Where are you headed?"

"Home I guess. I don't know. It's a sunny day out, and I have the rest of the day off. I thought a local could show me some hidden gems in the city before my time here ends."

"I can be there in twenty minutes. Fifteen if the traffic is light. What are you wearing?" His voice softened.

"Why?" I questioned, searching for the gumption to end the call.

"So I can know what to drive."

I was overcome with relief. "Jeans and boots," I said.

"See you in twenty. Meet me out front."

Lucas drove up a few minutes late on a motorcycle wearing a black leather jacket, dark blue denim, and work boots. He removed his helmet to show me his one dimple, flashing a smile I recognized all too well. *The fuck was I thinking?*

"Hop on." He lured me over to the bike.

"This was a mistake. Plus, I have reasons to live." I backed away.

"So do I. I promise I'm a safe driver. Let me help you with your helmet."

He stared into my eyes on and off as he tightened the notch on my protective head gear. I broke his gaze, crumbling inside I lacked the courage to walk away. *'This is the most reckless thing you can do,'* I thought to myself. *'Well since you shagged a man unprotected in three days, married him, and changed your life.'*

Caught up in the conversation taking place in my head, I mumbled out loud. "That turned out just fine."

"What did?" Lucas asked.

"Oh. Sorry. I was thinking out loud."

He grinned. "Let's go."

I held on tight to his chest as he wiggled in and out of traffic. Twenty minutes later, he introduced me to Brooklyn. "Word is, women love coming to the botanical gardens." He parked his bike, then lifted me to my feet.

I walked ahead of him, admiring the scenery of florals, asking myself if I held on to him too tight, was there a Freudian reason I called him, and how could I get out of the mess I created.

He caught up to me and suggested we warm up a bit at a café down the street. Over a latte we shared light conversation about his work in construction, looking at pictures on his phone of the buildings he built in and out the city. He was prouder than I was impressed.

When he realized he had been rambling, he joked. "You don't look interested at all in what I am saying."

"I'm sure it's exciting for you. The finished products are nice though."

"You don't have to be nervous around me. I won't bite."

"I hope not," I said. "Thanks for taking my call and showing me this side of town. I should probably catch a cab home."

"There's more I'd like to show. Please. Don't run off." He reached for my hand after placing a twenty between the sugar packets.

I ignored the signs and hopped back on his motorcycle, enjoying the view of a newly built hotspot called Dumbo. Boutiques, cobblestoned streets, market vendors, restaurants galore, and galleries brought in crowds of people from locals to tourists. It felt wrong I had stumbled on such a place with Lucas, and as we rode past a carousel near the Brooklyn Bridge on our way out, I created a speech to make sure Lucas and I never saw each other again.

He drove us to his place of work to defrost. A corner office overlooking the street from the third floor, well decorated with wood and plaques, with his name on the center of his shiny, chestnut coated desk. I studied his cockiness in his element, walking around as if he owned the place.

"Is it warm enough in here?" he asked.

"It's getting there. I'm thawing pretty nicely." I stood near the vent soaking up the heat.

"I ordered us some food. It should be here any minute."

"Thanks for showing me around today, but I really should get going. It's too late now, but I shouldn't have called you."

"I'm glad you did. I enjoyed your company this afternoon."

I scoffed. "When we met you asked me a million questions."

"And you refused to answer any of them."

"Now it's my turn. Why aren't you married?"

"I am. My wife lives in San Diego. Permanently, I hope."

"Trouble in paradise?" I teased.

"We're separated. There is no way I can leave this earth still married to her. She would get a pretty penny if my demise came before this divorce is final."

"What did you do to her?"

"I married her." He griped.

"Okaaaay. Why did you take me out today?"

"Because you asked me to."

"The real reason."

"I find you intriguing." He blushed.

"What is your intention with me, Mr. Fleming?"

"I think you know."

My eyes met his across the room. I grinned, folded my arms together, and looked back at the people and cars passing by on the street.

"I can help you get warm." He offered.

"I think the food is here."

Lucas sighed. "They would pick tonight to have fast delivery."

I laughed at his comment while he went downstairs to unlock

the entrance and grab the takeout. He returned and laid the bags on the table near the heating vent. I avoided eye contact with him as he spread the food across the shiny wood, and poured us some wine in coffee cups from his cabinet.

"How many women are you currently seeing, Mr. Fleming?"

"I have a few friends. But no one serious."

"Are you really married?"

"Separated. Why would I say I was if I wasn't?"

"I don't know. To maybe keep women from trying to get too close."

"I'm telling you the truth. I would be divorced if my ex wasn't fighting it so damn hard. You think you know a person."

He was convincing regarding the disdain for his wife, but I smelled bullshit about his innocence in the friends department.

"Shall we," he asked, pointing to the spread.

I sampled the lo-mein and raised my eyebrows. "The rumor is true."

"What's that?"

"New York has the best Chinese food."

He raised his head and looked down at me. "Nadia, what happens with us after tonight?"

"I go home, lose your number, and pretend this day never happened."

"I propose I drive you home. You invite me in..."

"Not going to happen."

"Then meet me for lunch tomorrow. I'll send a car and take you to eat the best steak New York has to offer."

"How about I think about it. And if I call you we can meet."

He rose from the table and went into the drawer of his desk. "Take this." He handed me a flip phone. "I had to fire someone today. This was his company phone. It's been wiped clean and has a new number. Expect it to ring tomorrow around eleven o'clock."

I placed the phone in my purse and called myself a taxi— proud I didn't misbehave though Lucas's craftiness made it tempting to play his game. Stimulated by control yet detached from commitment, I shamelessly flirted with him, knowing it was wrong because it felt good in doing so. As long as I remained mysterious I held all the cards, but as I stepped inside my apartment, the excitement of him left. And I promised myself not to ever see him again.

19

FOOLISH

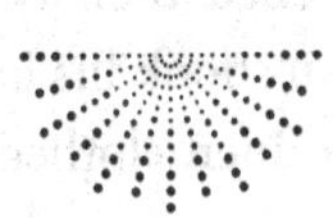

Walking down the hall of the studio a minute shy of eleven o'clock on the dot, the retro phone rang. I pulled it out of my bag and stared at it for a few seconds. A crew member I'd spoken to once or twice frowned at the device in my hand, then I laughed along with him until he turned the corner.

I let the line ring a few more times, then answered the call chuckling.

"What's so funny?" Lucas asked.

"The look on this guy's face when he saw I had a flip phone."

"I couldn't exactly call your phone, could I?"

"You're so relentless. Are you calling me to cancel, or give me an address?"

"I know this is a stretch, but tell me where you are. I'll send a car."

"That won't be wise."

"Then come to the office. We'll leave from here."

Lucas stood out front when the cab delivered me to another wrong move on my part. He opened the door of a town car for me, and whisked me off to a lunch date in style. He was a sight in gray. His broad shoulders perfectly filled the charcoal jacket he wore, and the imprint in his trousers was hard to miss. His big light brown eyes seduced me in silence, to the point I was forced to look away, peeping at him in spurts, blushing of nervousness.

We arrived at a restaurant on 57th street, with a huge wooden door and a sign nailed into it that read, *'Hours 5 p.m. to 1 a.m.'* Lucas made a call and the door opened, then locked immediately upon our entry. A short red-faced man shook his hand, and kissed the back of mine, then ushered us to a linen clothed table in the center of the room.

He returned with a bottle of champagne and placed it between us. I was impressed at the length he went to succeed in getting me to fall for him.

"A man of many connections, I see."

He held his head high. "In my line of work, relationships are important."

"Apparently. Any recommendations?"

"Whatever cut you select will be amazing. Feel free to try whatever you like."

I ordered the mignon medium-well with a side salad and baked sweet potato. He ordered the prime rib with mashed potatoes, and an appetizer of stuffed shrimp he insisted I try. The shrimp were so succulent and tender I wanted them all to myself.

"Amazing, right?" He grinned.

"The best I've ever had."

"Wait until the steaks arrive. I might get you to call my name after all."

I guffawed lowly at his inappropriateness. "I beg your pardon."

Lucas acted as if he didn't hear me and poured us both a glass of champagne.

I sipped a little. "I can't have much. I have to report back to work."

He raised his hand signaling he understood. "Say when."

Our lunch arrived and the room went completely silent, minus the sounds of us devouring our feast. Conversation picked back up between us as we sampled from each other's plate.

"If you tell me about your marriage, I'll tell you about mine."

He agreed.

"What went wrong?" I asked him.

He set his fork on the table. "So many things. I remember she grew upset on our honeymoon because I called her my girlfriend and not my wife. Easy mistake as a newlywed, but she went bananas. Completely shut down on me."

"What do you mean shut down?"

"No sex. It was our honeymoon, and she used an honest mistake as a reason to withdraw intimacy."

"No nookie on your honeymoon seems a bit extreme."

"Tell me about it. I called her my girlfriend for three years. Simple slip of the tongue. The next morning, I knew I had made a mistake, but I went along with the 'for better or worse part'. She woke up and acted as if nothing happened."

I held my hand over my mouth to cover the food processing inside. Gasping for air, and swallowing at the same time I snorted. "I'm sorry to laugh. It's not funny. But the way you tell it is funny. And I'm guilty of shutting down myself, but not for something as small as being called girlfriend."

"Good to know. The next nine months I was on pins and needles trying not to say the wrong thing. I was miserable. And let's not talk about me going to hang out with my boys. She would flip out. I was like where was this person before I wasted money on feeding people who didn't give a damn if we stayed together or not. Anyway, when we hit the one-year mark I filed for divorce, and she has hated me ever since. She won't comply with the terms, and is fighting me at every turn. I want out. Now tell me about you Ms. Full of Secrets."

"There isn't much to tell. My husband didn't want me to come to New York for this job I'm working."

"That's the complication you speak of?"

I nodded yes.

"I was hoping for a bit more, or a real piece of information about you. Like your last name. Where are you from? What movies do you like? Your favorite book? That sort of thing. Let me in a little. How long have you been married?"

"A little over two years."

"Still fairly new. They say marriage is an institution and they mean it. You learn something new every day like you're in school. About yourself and your mate."

"Spoken like a true person burned by the institute." I joked.

He laughed to himself. "You're witty. I know that about you."

He stared at me with ill intent written across his face. I was enjoying a meal with a man who wanted to rip my clothes off, feeling guilty every second knowing it by the way he looked at me. And I liked the torture. The desire in his gaze. The power I felt owning his attention.

He interrupted my introspection. "How are you enjoying married life?"

"I enjoy it actually."

"Have you and your mate figured each other out?"

"I'd say yes. I was lonely and heartbroken before him. Now it feels good to have someone to go through life with as an ally. We just have to work on straightening out a few wrinkles, but who doesn't? That's life."

"If I may, exactly where do I fall in line with what you have going on?" He stopped eating.

"I'm not quite sure. I thought we could be friends. But you've already expressed sleeping with me, and I'm not a cheating woman."

He wiped his mouth with the linen cloth, then leaned forward. "You're doing so in this very moment."

I swallowed a tiny sip of champagne and sat back in my chair. "I disagree."

"Cheating doesn't have to be physical, though in this case I would like it to. Very much so. And you won't admit it, but you want to sleep with me just as bad as I want to ravish your body into sweet submission and hear you call my name. But as you said, you aren't a cheating woman. And I believe you."

I was cornered. I had imagined what he would be like in the sack. How his lips would feel against mine, and if he had something new to offer I had yet to experience. I had no intention of ever finding out, but the images flashed before me as he said the words.

He grinned at me as if he knew what I was thinking. I grinned back at him as the server returned with a to go order of the shrimp prepared in a brown box, and a slice of banana fosters cake sitting pretty inside a clear tray.

"I knew you would love them so I ordered one for you to have for your dinner tonight." He spread five one hundred-dollar bills on the table.

"Thank you, my clever associate." I sampled the icing from the cake.

"Associate?" He mumbled, gazing at me hard as I licked my finger. "Oh, how I wish you'd call me lover instead."

We spent the remaining minutes staring at each other as the owner stood above with an invitation to return for dinner. The car arrived and drove us back to his office.

Lucas hesitated getting out. "Come away with me this weekend."

Tension in my legs rose and I stuttered. "I can't."

"Why not?"

"I have friends flying in this weekend."

"How about next weekend?"

"Lucas. I'm married."

"Think about it okay? And keep the phone turned on. I'll be calling you."

The car dropped me off a block away from the studio as I requested. I trekked down the concrete smiling to myself like the girl on the train I admired my first week in Manhattan. I didn't know her story, but I knew mine, and it was messy. *'What the fuck had I gotten myself into?'*

20

FRIENDS

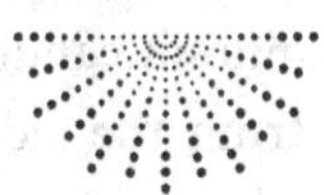

The arrival of Khai and Shannon timed perfectly with my drama. Shannon, the devil on my shoulder, and Khai the angel, brought the much-needed camaraderie missing from my life.

Our sisterhood was cracked. I barely spoke to them for months, and found myself closer to Olive during the turmoil, but the minute they learned I was on home soil, they jumped at the chance to mend what was broken.

To prepare for their visit, I blew up the floor mattress and stocked the cabinets with liquor, wine, and snacks. I missed them so much, I met them curbside when they texted their cab turned on my block. We hugged and screamed on the sidewalk, easily picking up where we left off.

"Before we go inside, you should know the apartment is nothing like the house in London."

Khai looked around my empty space. "I'm not going to ask how much this small place costs because I already know it's a fortune with a doorman sitting downstairs."

"It's cute. And clean of course." Shannon critiqued.

"Now that the disappointment is out of the way, who's sleeping with who? We have the sofa, the blow-up mattress, or someone can sleep with me."

"What's wrong with you?" Khai asked me. "Your eyes have a funny look about them."

"You guys just got here. We'll talk about it once you get settled in."

"Settled in?" Shannon laughed. "Bitch, we here? Spill the tea."

My face grimaced at Shannon's candor. "I missed you a lot. You know that?" I hugged her from the side. "Now, first things first. What do you two want to get into?"

Shannon surprised both Khai and I. "I am down to stay in the house tonight, hang back, and hear this tea. Thirty ain't so flirty."

Khai looked over to me. "This is who we've become. Scary right?"

I nodded in disbelief and slouched my shoulders, then plopped down on the couch. "Well, we can scratch off going to this nice bar I found where the music is on point, and the vibe is real mellow."

"Are you talking about the spot you were in the other night when I called?"

My face simpered of guilt.

"Were there any cute guys there?" Shannon asked.

"You won't find any Yohan's in there. Speaking of Han,

I can't be a part of your creeping with him. I'm cool with Olive now, and it doesn't feel right. Especially when he asks me about you using code language. I feel like I'm in on it."

Shannon sat next to me on the sofa and laid her head in my lap. "He's keeping tabs on me huh?"

I rolled her off of me. "Not like that."

She lashed into me. "I told you not to be friends with her. Should I gather my things and go to a hotel?" Shannon threatened.

"The last thing I need is to fight with you Sha. I have enough on my plate— But you know you and him were supposed to be a one and done."

"I can't help it if your boss prefers this Americanized ass over a boring stiff." She squeezed me and laughed. "Now, what did you mean by you have a lot on your plate? You and The Iceman Cometh having problems?"

"No. Nothing like that."

"Good. Because I'm walking the plank in six weeks, and you're both in the wedding. You'll still be in the states, so it all works out for my shower and bachelorette party. I also need you to fix this business with Taylor before I walk down the aisle so we can have a good time."

"I can be cordial to Taylor, but why are you playing around with Yohan when you've set a date?"

"There's nothing wrong with talking? Yohan is over there and I'm over here. And as for you and Taylor, being cordial is not good enough. I want things to be like they used to be, without the tension in the group."

I scoffed. "The best I can do is be cool. No drama."

Shannon raised her hand. "Do either of you hear a buzzing noise?"

My eyes grew big.

"It's coming from over there." Khai pointed to my purse.

"But your phone is in your hand." Shannon side-eyed me and we wrestled charging towards my purse. "Oh shit! Nadia you running the two-phone game?"

"Get your hands out of my stuff!"

Shannon pinned me to the ground.

"You've got Shannon on the line. Who is this?"

"Hi." Lucas's voice vibrated through the phone. "You must be one of the friends flying in for the weekend."

"So, you've heard of us." Shannon twisted her mouth.

"I have. Is Nadia available?"

Shannon held the phone next to both of our ears.

"Hey Lucas. What's up?" I sighed.

"I was wondering if you wanted to bring your friends down to the spot tonight?"

"Thanks, but we're staying in tonight."

Shannon talked over me. "We would love to join you, Lucas."

"Cool. I'll be there in an hour. See you then."

"You might not!" I shouted as the call ended.

Shannon giggled as she rolled off of me. Khai stood above us and reached for my hand. She pulled me from the floor, judging me hard like a school teacher in front of a class.

Shannon pinched me. "Bitch get dressed. You have some explaining to do."

I gave the girls the rundown on how Lucas came about, and how I ended up with the flip phone. Shannon did her normal routine of google searching people online, and checked out his profile.

"I'm glad he got to you first sis, because I would leave my fiancé for a man this fine."

"He's okay. Looks aren't everything." I rolled my eyes.

"Says the *sistah* with the white chocolate man giving her the world, and judging by these numbers a caramel macchiato who can almost do the same." Shannon reported.

Khai chimed in. "Self-sabotaging are we, Nadia?"

"It's all innocent. He's just a friend."

"Married women don't need male friends. What's really going on between you and Mash?"

On the way to the bar, I filled them in about the dreaded ex, his undead father, and our rift before I came to New York. As expected, Khai weighed in as the unlicensed group therapist.

"It's okay to be confused, Nadia. The backstabbing of a close friend, the ex-girlfriend who won't go away, and the pain Dylan caused you is still affecting you. Add on a misunderstanding with your husband, and your obsessive need to hold onto things, I'm not surprised you're up here about to fuck your shit up."

"Damn Iyanla. You 'gon call her beloved next?" Shannon joked.

I chortled. "Did I mention the man who put his arm around me in Paris is his dad?"

"Shut up!" Shannon shoved my arm.

"Nadia, you can stop this. You're using this Lucas person to prove a point." Khai stared me down.

"It's cool to look at the menu, just don't order from it." Shannon added. "Good morning Mr. Sharper is the man for you." Her tongue hung from the side of her mouth as she wound her hips on the seat, mocking me from her prior visit.

I looked ahead and held in my laugh. "You're not going to let me live that down, are you?"

"Never." She kissed my cheek.

Khai passed me a tissue to clean the lipstick from my cheek. I led the girls to the bar and introduced them to Lucas and Al.

"Remember me?" I flashed Al a smile.

"Good to see you. My friend here can't stop talking about you. He finally got you back in here for your special drink?" Al wiped the rim of a glass, glancing at my friends.

"Special drink?" Shannon pinched my ass. "You're like a totally different person up here."

"We'll have 3 specialties, Al."

"Bitch you keeping secrets like a *mufucka*. Who are you? Me?" Shannon questioned.

"Just shut up and tell me if you like it."

Shannon and Khai gave each other a once over, then sipped the mauve colored concoction.

Lucas smiled at Al. "Keep these coming, Al. Ladies, follow me," he said, leading us to a booth upstairs overlooking the stage. He looked at me. "I wouldn't put you in that hot seat."

Shannon whispered in my ear. "Bitch, I want all the tea."

I tittered to myself, grooving to the band, and table dancing with the girls, guzzling every drink Al sent to us. Khai cut off the final round of drinks.

"You've had one too many," she said.

"Why you say that?" I leaned on her shoulder.

"You're laughing at everything this man says. He's good looking, but not funny."

"He's not?"

She shook her head side to side.

"Ladies, I hired a driver for the night. Can I interest you three beauties in a midnight tour of the city?"

"We'd love to," I said.

Shannon sat in the front seat, flirting with the driver. I sat in the back seat between Lucas and Khai. We rode past The Apollo Theatre, admired the lights and billboards while stuck in traffic near Times Square, then foolishly froze in the cold for a drunken photo in front of the bridge.

Lucas mentioned his apartment was nearby. Khai sat stone-faced in the car when Shannon and I agreed we wanted to see it. He gave us the tour of the recreation room on the bottom floor. Equipped with a jacuzzi, swimming pool, and fitness area. Then he welcomed us into his luxury pad.

"Why are we here again?" Khai asked.

"I hope it's so we can get in the jacuzzi?" Shannon asked.

"I think we should call it a night." Khai glared at Lucas.

"I have several rooms, and you're welcome to stay here for the night. We could order in, get in the jacuzzi if you like. The pool is also heated by the way."

"We don't have bathing suits," Khai replied.

Shannon in a drunken stupor didn't catch Khai's vibe. "I wish I had mine. I'd go downstairs and smoke on something in the jacuzzi."

"I'll send the driver to get you one." Lucas pulled out his phone.

"At this time of night?" Shannon raised her brows.

"You're in New York City baby."

The driver drove us to the closest general store. Lucas offered to pay for the goods.

Khai pushed his card away. "No thank you. We aren't broke bitches."

"I'm just being a good host," he said.

"Um huh." Khai hummed.

Back at Lucas's, Khai begged me not to get changed. "Trust me this one time," she said. And I did. I sat next to Lucas in the lounge chairs while she and Shannon soaked in the water and sipped champagne.

"Why did you change your mind about getting in?" he asked me.

"I'm a little tipsy. Not really up for it. Why don't you get in?"

"I would if you were in there." His russet eyes gleamed at me.

"Hey Lucas." Khai snapped her fingers. "Did Nadia tell you she's married?"

"She did."

"To a good man. A man we all love and approve of. I'm not knocking you down to size, because you are undoubtedly doing good for yourself, and seem to be a nice guy, but her man loves her. Like a lot."

He looked back at me. "And she loves him. She's made that clear."

"Good, so what's the real reason you brought us here?"

He bowed his head. "Okay, you got me. I was having a good time with you ladies, and I didn't want the night to end. I brought you here to keep me company. There you have it. The truth."

"He's also married." I told them.

"Waiting for my divorce to be final." He corrected me. "And to lower any red flags, Nadia has been clear about our friendship from the beginning."

"Don't take this the wrong way Lucas, *but er ugh*, sis." Shannon waved her finger at me. "Don't sleep with this man. He is smooth. I sense trouble a-brewing between you two."

"We should go." Khai stepped out of the water.

While the girls changed in one of the spare rooms, I sat with Lucas on the loveseat in his living room. He picked up a remote from the coffee table and dimmed the lights above us, then reached down and placed my feet in his lap. He removed my left boot and ran his knuckles up and down the ball of my foot.

"Your feet are freezing."

"They always are." A tingle shot up my spine.

"Do you want a pair of my socks? They are thick."

"That would be nice." I kicked off my other boot.

He returned with a pair of fresh white knee socks and a blanket from his room, rolled the socks up to my calves and covered me.

"What's with the blanket?"

"Your friends are asleep."

"I knew they were taking too long."

"It's cool. I've wanted a moment alone with you all night."

'Dammit,' I thought to myself.

"I should go wake them." I kicked the blanket off of me.

"It'll be morning soon enough." His hands squeezed my feet.

"Lucas, a moment alone can lead to complications. Shannon's the single one. She should be out here with you. Not me."

"She's not my type." He bent my toes back and forth.

"But she's DTF." I gasped lightly.

He smiled at me. "Feels good?"

I nodded.

"A down to fuck woman doesn't turn me on. You do. A smart man knows when you lay with a woman, she is yours for thirty days."

"Thirty days? I'm afraid I don't follow."

"You know. Thirty days to see if you've planted a seed."

My cheeks rosed as I thought, 'That's some real heaux boy shit to say.'

"Therefore, I choose wisely. I choose you."

"Do you have children?"

"A daughter back home in Seattle." He confessed, then deflected. "Are you comfortable?"

"I'm fine. I won't get any sleep tonight. Can't sleep in an unfamiliar place."

"I'm the same way. Looks like we're in for an all-nighter. Here." He handed me the remote. "You pick the movie."

I excused myself to the guest bedroom to shake the shit out of

Shannon and Khai. One was half dressed with one shoe on, and the other still wrapped in a towel hugged up with a pillow.

I returned to the living room. "If we stay here, are you going to tie us up, and kill us in the middle of the night?"

"The tying you up part sounds nice, but other than that I wouldn't hurt a fly." He smiled, then passed me the remote.

Spoken like a true serial killer.

I strolled the lists on his apps and searched for a war movie to kill any romance vibes. He caught on to what I was doing so he switched to his monthly subscription channel, and suggested we watch a limited series. I chose one about crime. Murder and mistrust would easily kill the sexual tension in the room.

We sat through the first episode mesmerized at the storyline. By episode 2 he nodded off, and episode 3 took me down shortly after.

I jumped up an hour or so later when his hands gripped my feet. The program was now on episode 5, and I had no idea what was going on with the story arc. I escaped his grasp and snuck back into the room with the girls. I nudged Khai as I finished dressing her. She was out for the count. Shannon talked to me out of her head, pushing me away as I attempted to put her other shoe on. Then she snored like a bear, so I covered her with a corner of the comforter, and tiptoed back into the living room.

Lucas sat upright, changing the program to the news. "Is everything alright?"

I sat down on my end of the chair. "Yeah, just checking on my girls."

"I'm sorry I fell asleep on you. Come here. Sit closer to me." He patted the cushion.

I slid over an inch. "Who keeps you company at night?"

Lucas set the alarm on his phone and placed it on the coffee table. "Work. I haven't been able to focus on anyone with this impending divorce. I told you I have friends, but I'm not seeing anyone exclusively. If I were, she'd be here right now."

"I find that hard to believe."

The room fell silent. I placed my feet on the couch with both knees bent staring at the television, big-eyed and uneasy, struggling to stay awake. We watched the news, nodding off in shifts. Then, my head fell on his arm and I jumped. He wrapped it around me, and I squirmed. It felt strange to have another man's hands touch my skin. The hairs on my arm lifted as I sensed he was no longer asleep, and looking down at me. I kept my head turned towards the television, but that wasn't enough to deter Lucas from getting what he wanted.

He removed his arm and kissed my temple. I shivered and froze all at once. He leaned further down and gently kissed the side of my face, turning my chin towards him to taste his lips. I opened my mouth. "I can't," I said. He caught me on the inhale, and held his lips on top of mine. I puckered up and kissed him back, then pulled away.

He opened his eyes. "I knew it."

"You knew what." I turned my head.

"You wanted me, too." He grabbed my chin and turned my face towards him.

"Lucas, I'm not this woman."

"I know you aren't. I can tell. But I just couldn't help myself." He sat back on the couch, wrapped his arms around me, leaned his head back on the sofa, and this time went to sleep.

I removed his arm and slid to the opposite end of the couch, disheveled in my thoughts. One minute I was kicking myself, the next smiling. I listened to Lucas grunt in his sleep until the alarm rang. He turned it off, sat back and grinned to himself.

"Did I dream that?"

I didn't respond.

"Did you get any sleep?" he asked.

"Maybe an hour."

"I need to take a shower and get ready for a long day on site. You need anything?"

"I'm good. Can you ask the driver to warm the car? I'm going to wake the girls."

"Consider it done. It won't take me long."

I pinched Khai and Shannon until they woke up. They begged for five more minutes to sleep, dozing off regardless of my pricking their skin. Five minutes turned into ten minutes. Lucas hadn't returned to the living room. I knocked on his room door. "Come in." He granted.

I opened the door. *Have mercy.* "Kings and Queens," I mumbled.

"Say what?"

"Ugh, nothing. I was just remembering a lecture someone gave me." I couldn't look away at him standing in all of his glory.

"Sounds like you said Kings and Queens."

I did an about face.

He pulled me back inside. "Tell me what it means."

"Could you put some shorts on?"

He fumbled around in his chest drawer.

I hid my face below my palm. "The girls are moving slow. Can we hang back, and lock up when we leave?"

"If you promise not to rob me." He joked. "Of course. I trust you." He approached me with his undergarments thrown across his shoulder.

"Shannon was right. You are trouble."

He lifted me up and placed my legs around his. I felt like I was helping him maneuver me, but at the same time still as a broken clock. He kissed me like he meant it this time. Tongue bathing my mouth until I exhaled the guilt mixed with desire rushing inside of me. I kissed him back, wanting to stop, but weak from the sensation tingling in my pussy now controlling my mind.

Lucas carried me around his waist to the side of the door and began to close it when I snapped out of delirium.

I hopped down and put my hand between the crack. "What the fuck have I done?"

He pressed against me and stared in my eyes, overflowing with lust I couldn't handle. "What needs to be done." He whispered. "It'll be great. You and I both know it."

I looked down and sighed at the monstrous, onyx lumber the constructionist packed. "Oh hell no, Lucas." My mouth watered.

"Kiss me one more time. Please." He begged.

In weakness, lust, and depravation of touch I agreed. "Just one more."

His dick nearly pierced my upper abdomen. I placed my hands on his chest. His heart was beating a hundred miles a minute as his cock contracted against my sweater. He reached to close the door again, and I stopped.

"Okay, that's enough. Lucas you will ruin me. I see why your wife doesn't want to let you go." I slid between the crack of the door.

"Don't ruin the moment talking about her. This is about you and me."

"There can't be a you and me." I pushed him off and walked out.

"Let me get dressed so we can talk about this."

"I'll call you later. We'll talk then." I rushed into the room with the girls.

I shook the shit out of Khai and Shannon until they woke up. Shannon cursed me, ready to fight.

"Grab your shit and let's roll now," I commanded.

Khai held her head. "What's wrong?"

"It's a code California." I emphasized strongly.

"California! Oh shit," said Shannon. "I said look at the menu. Don't taste from it!"

"I didn't taste, but I sampled the appetizer. We gotta go. Now!"

We scrambled for our things, jetted out of the front door, and fled into the car waiting out front.

"Nadia, what the hell man? Code California?" Khai shook her head.

"No talking in the car. Let's get home first." I shushed them, and instructed the driver to let us out a block away from my apartment.

We walked the short distance and entered the lobby looking like last night's havoc, napped for two hours, then woke for our brunch reservation at The Regent.

To mask my racoon eyes, I piled on makeup and wore sunglasses even though the sun wasn't out. The girls followed suit, and on the way to the hotel, I filled them in with what transpired.

"We haven't had to use code California since California," said Shannon. "When you say you sampled you don't mean oral transaction do you? 'Cause if you do, then you may as well have *ate* from every section."

"Jesus Christ Shannon, we only kissed. And I saw him naked."

"He kissed you, or you kissed him?" Khai asked.

"He initiated and I didn't stop him. Twice or thrice. It's all a blur. I'm so ashamed."

"How was it?" Shannon's voice lowered seductively.

"It was nice. Different but nice. It happened so fast and it was over quick, I don't know. Goodness I was dripping wet. What's wrong with me?" I whined.

"You're human. And I told you, you were self-sabotaging." Khai grabbed my hand. "But how did you see his dick?"

"When he was getting out of the shower."

Shannon fake coughed and cleared her throat. "Details please."

I smiled at both of them and took their hands. "The man could be on a poster. Face, body, and wood. I actually told him he would ruin me."

Shannon stared into space and Khai bit her fingernails while I smiled to myself. The driver grinned in the rear-view mirror, and shared a grin with me.

"If I had to say, the man has damaged many a womb."

Shannon slapped my arm. "We were in the house with a thick hog, and you cock blocked us from jumping on it."

"Shannon please." Khai hushed her. "These next six weeks can't get here fast enough. Nadia, I'm proud of you. You did good to walk away. Especially since I don't know if I could have. The man was tempting. I think I even dreamed about him last night."

"Whaaaaat!" Shannon and I blurted out together.

"Blame the alcohol." Khai tooted up her lips. "I mean I find other men attractive all the time. I just don't act on it."

Shannon's nostrils flared when I leaned up to look at her. Khai's confession shocked us into silence during the rest of the car ride.

Finding the eatery inside the maze of a hotel was a hard task for hungover, sleep deprived newbies to the big city. Once we found the café holding our reservation, Khai gave the maître de her last name, and he escorted us to our reserved table.

I stopped in my tracks and grunted. "You bitches."

21

TALK ABOUT IT

I was ambushed. Taylor and Isla sat with their backs to the wall, locking eyes with me the moment we turned the corner. I took a step back and the girls shoved me forward with whispered obscenities and threats.

"I'll never forgive you two for this. And not a word about last night." I gritted through my teeth.

"It's in the vault." Shannon assured me.

I clicked my teeth, then sat down across from the backstabbing duo. Taylor stood and extended her arms to me. I raised both of my brows and looked at her like she was crazy.

"As promised, we got Nadia here," said Khai. "She agreed to be cordial, so let's keep it rated G ladies."

Taylor sat down. "It's good to see you, Nadia."

"I'm glad you're doing well," I replied. "But I won't be forced into anything."

"I didn't think you would still be this angry with me. So much time has passed, I was hoping we could work this out. I truly am sorry for hurting you. If I could take it back I would."

"No, you wouldn't. It would be un-Taylor-like to not do whatever she wanted no matter the cost. I just have to know. Who pursued who?" I swayed my head and tucked my lips.

She paused and looked around the table. "He did. At one of the game nights. You two were having problems, and he said something I didn't take serious at first, but then you broke up and he approached me at a gas station saying he needed someone to talk to. He started calling me at work and then one day showed up at my job around the time I was pissed with Levi because he was still talking to his ex. I went out with Dylan to even the score, but you know how he is, and I gave in. But I promise we never snuck around when you two were together." She raised her hand to scout's honor.

I didn't believe her, but for the sake of us being in public I maintained my cool. "Here's my dilemma. I'm married so I'm in the position where I'm not supposed to care what, or who my ex-boyfriend is doing. My feelings are invalid in all of this, yet they are very real. Not for Dylan, but for one of my best friends making me look and feel like a fool."

"Nadia, I never..."

"I keep thinking about how you clowned me at your shower. Remember that? Teasing me. Saying I was still hung up on Dylan, and you were fucking him the entire time, and laughing at me in my face."

The girls mumbled and adjusted their seating.

"I don't hear anyone speaking up on my behalf. Have I said anything untrue?" I said to the table.

"You're hitting all the main points." Khai and Shannon cosigned.

"I don't trust you, Taylor. I will never think of you as my friend, and this ambush was a waste of time. But I wish you well."

"So that's it. You're just going to cut me out of your life?"

"You handed me the scissors." I pushed my seat back.

Khai grabbed my hand and gestured I sit back down. My shoulders slumped as I scooted my chair closer to the table.

"Wow, Nadia. You're sitting over there like you're all perfect." Taylor tapped on the table.

"I'm far from it. But looking at you, I see the kind of person I don't want to be. So, thank you, and know I forgive you. Dylan is your problem now."

I turned to Isla. "Since my ex boyfriends are the hot ticket item, how is Evan doing?"

"We're no longer..." Isla stuttered.

"You two are exactly alike." I added.

"Nadia, for my family's sake, we need to find a way we can get past this." Taylor pled.

"Family's sake?" Shannon questioned.

"Yes. Levi is on my case day and night wondering what happened between us."

"Well I'm not going to lie to him on your behalf, Taylor. It's why I have avoided speaking with him."

Eyes shifted from both ends of the table.

Khai asked the hard-hitting questions. "I thought everyone knew you had the affair with Dylan. But a moment ago, Nadia said he was your problem. If the affair is over, why is he still your problem?"

I raised my brows and scoffed. Taylor shook as tears fell from her eyes. She squeezed her hands together so tight they turned red.

"Yes, Dylan and I had an affair. But he is also Tyler's father." She confessed, then glared at me. "How did you know?"

"Your question confirms that Dylan is still a piece of shit and full of secrets." I chuckled. "I sat with you while you were sick. I read the card stuck inside the flowers he sent, and trashed it before Levi saw it. Yeah. That was me looking out for my friends. Then, he snuck into your room and told me everything. I love Levi like a brother, and won't ever tell him, because he's suffered quite a lot by your hands. You just better hope Dylan stays quiet."

"And everyone at this table." Taylor begged.

The girls locked their lips and promised not to expose Taylor's secret as our waitress finally arrived to take our order. As she walked away, Isla threw insults.

"Why do you three look like shit this morning?"

We eyed one another and burst into laughter, then removed our sunglasses to reveal the dark circles and bags.

"We went out last night and haven't slept," said Khai.

Shannon opened her trap as usual and said too much. "A hot guy flashed his shaboynka to Nadia last night, and it's all she could talk about on the way over here. You know it's been a few years since she's had a chocolate one in her face."

I looked at her like a deer caught in headlights as the entire table laughed at me like old times.

"What did it look like?" Isla asked.

"Like Michael Jackson singing on Christmas morning," I blurted.

The table roared, attracting unwanted attention and glares. We lowered our voices and snickered like we did when we were close.

"I miss this guys," said Isla. "Taylor isn't the only one who crossed the line. I did, too. Nadia, I'm sorry. I was jealous of you and Mash. And the joke was on me trying to date Evan. His ass was whack like you said."

I smiled at Isla for the first time in years. "I heard you were hummus shopping, too."

She blushed. "I tried it, but he didn't get our culture at all. I prefer being with a brother. They get me." She held her chest.

"Yes, my white chocolate is one of a kind." I boasted.

"Oh shit." Shannon leaned into the table and whispered. "Did y'all hear it?"

"I did." Khai and Isla tittered.

"So did I." Taylor chuckled.

"What?" I asked.

"You had a little British twang mixed in with your country grammar." Shannon teased. "Say it again."

"Y'all can go to hell."

"There it is again!"

We laughed together at my expense, and Shannon used the moment to unite us for her wedding.

"Doesn't this feel good y'all. We'll be doing it again in six weeks, and I want us to be just like this."

My phone interrupted her speech. "Excuse me for a second," I said, and left the table. "Hey. I'm with the girls. I have to tell you what happened."

"I have news also." Mash announced. "The house sold for fifty thousand dollars less than our asking price, but the new house in Richmond had an offer of $850,000.00 more than we invested from a buyer. You said you wanted to flip houses, so I accepted the offer. We'll be in the flat a little longer."

"I have no problem with that. Any chance I'll see you again before Shannon's wedding? It's in six weeks by the way, and you're in it."

"We can make it happen. Get back to your friends. Levi already told me Taylor was up there. I'm on your side, and I love you."

I returned to the table and suggested instead of clubbing, we all hang out together at my place, or their hotel room for the night.

"Does this mean you forgive me?" Taylor asked.

"It means, we're hanging out and we'll see where it takes us."

The night became reminiscent of the old days when we were five friends, and thick as thieves, figuring out our paths in life. It was the stepping stone to rekindling a fraction of my friendship with Taylor, and the first step in healing from the pain she inflicted upon me. Just what the doctor ordered.

22

HOLLOW DISPLAY

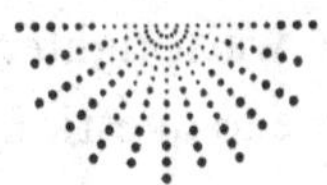

I lied to Lucas when I said I would get back to him. Flashes of his hands touching my face haunted me in the middle of the night, though there were times I found myself smiling at the thought of him.

The girls had been gone for two weeks, and in those weeks, I couldn't get him off of my mind. I powered down his phone, and placed it on the top shelf in the kitchen, all the way in the back. For damage control, I took matters into my own hands and surprised Mash at his concert in Berlin.

His song with Essence was charting big numbers, leading to nonstop shows throughout Europe, and with Gemma's help, I popped up on the side of the stage where I belonged.

Mash skipped the after show and we raced to the hotel. We stumbled, tripped, and staggered into his room, sucking on each other against the wall. I had to taste him. I needed to taste him. I kissed, licked, sucked and gagged on his shaft, erasing the image of Lucas from my mind until the scent of Maximus stained the tip of my tongue and nose.

Needing that hit of coital elation when our flesh collided, I suggested an act we never explored. "Choke me," I said. Mash looked concerned at first, but went with it in the heat of the moment. I accepted it as punishment for my wrongdoing, holding my breath when I climaxed with his hands around my neck. The peak of it was explosive and intense, bringing us closer through touch. The pit— it didn't feel like I was being punished. I thoroughly enjoyed it.

The exploration of our strangulation asphyxiation wore me down. Mash held me by the waist tighter than he did my neck. The guilt I carried with me led me to question him.

"Has what's her face been to any of the shows I missed?"

His grip around my waist softened, and he paused longer than I liked. "I saw her in the crowd once. She didn't approach me or anything though."

"So, the restraining order was a flippant threat, huh?" I squirmed from beneath his sweaty arm. "Were you going to tell me if I didn't ask?"

"I didn't speak to her, and we're not doing this right now. You didn't fly out here to argue with me about someone who is of no importance, and I didn't spend the last hour making you call my name to ruin it with meaningless conversation. I love you."

I took his answer as a no and gave up the argument. He assumed he talked his way out of having to confess he wouldn't have told me she was still hanging around on standby. I lied in his arms wondering, *'What is with those two? She threatens to go to the tabloids if she doesn't get what she wants, and he threatens a restraining order if she doesn't go away. But neither of them act on their warning. I'm truly sick of this shit.'*

Another round of mind-blowing sex I flew around the world for was enough to tide me over, and put the issue on pause. I threw my pussy on him so hard I thought I broke it the morning after my flight home, keeled over in pain from a bladder infection.

The matter sorted out with meds, and over the course of four weeks left in the Big Apple, I did everything to avoid making the same mistake again. I kept busy with Italian lessons and ballet classes through the week, and travelled out of the city on the weekends.

I flew into Charlotte and GSP for two weekends in a row. Getting fatter every day of my visits. I worked off the home cooked meals from mom, the dining out, and alcoholic binges with the girls in the fitness center on the basement floor of my building.

As the countdown was near its end, I took one final flight into Charleston to spend some time with Grams. I rented a car and drove her everywhere she wanted to go, including the beach in the middle of winter. The temperature wasn't nearly as freezing as it was in the north, but the forceful winds shortened our time spent on the shore.

Collecting sea shells stuck in the sand, Grams gave me more life lessons.

"I thought a lot about what you said on my last visit, Grams."

"I hoped you would."

"And I met someone." I confessed.

"I assume he is handsome. The devil always is." Grams clicked her tongue and winked at me.

"Very." I nodded. "And now I'm confused. How is it possible to be in love with someone, but thinking of someone else?"

"Easy. You love one, and you like the other. Just because you're married doesn't mean you won't find anyone else attractive. You still have eyes."

"So, what do I do?"

"Well your situation is different from most. In my day the majority of men were assholes. They felt entitled, because you know, women didn't have many rights. We were always looked at as maids, and property, and told to be submissive. Women like me who weren't putting up with the bullshit had it even harder. Nowadays, there are some men who actually respect women and see them as their equal. Even worship the ground they walk on. Like your husband. He calls me you know."

"I didn't know. Since when?"

"Since my party. But he calls me more often since you took this job you're doing. He loves you, and I don't think it's an act. He is afraid of losing you."

I looked out into the ocean while Grams shared her conversations with Mash. I felt bad for flirting with Lucas. Allowing him to place his arm around me on the sofa. Holding on to him on the back of his motorcycle. The kiss. That menacing gotdamned kiss.

"Now I know I told you to have a back-up man, but in your case, you're pretty enough to get one in your old age if you need one." Grams touched my nose. "Look at me. I have three, and I don't know what to do with any of them. Chile forget about what I said. My generation is my generation, and yours has evolved. Two different times, two different set of rules."

"Now I feel guilty. I mean things never got physical, but I have thought about it several times. I've avoided the other man for weeks because I'm afraid I'll give into temptation."

"And you haven't because you love your husband, and are loyal like your mother. I don't think this other fella could love you the way you are loved right now. Now if it were me, I would have jumped that man's bones, and went on like nothing happened. But I digress."

We shared a good laugh and headed back to the car. "Nadia, you did good gal. I'm proud of ya. Take heed to my word, and call it off with that other fella. Ya hear me?"

"Yes ma'am. I will. I'll call him when I get back and end it civilly."

"Civilly. Right. Now if you ever feel something isn't right in your bones, trust that feeling and do what you have to do. Remember a rat has more than one hole to go to."

I flew out in the morning and returned to the cold where I exercised two, sometimes three times a day. If I was too tired to exercise I wrote, or searched for submissions to find my next gig. Still mustering up the courage to face Lucas.

I stood on the edge of the counter and retrieved the phone from the cabinet. I powered it on and crossed my fingers that my ghosting him helped to kill the sexual tension between us, and revealed an ugly side of him to make him easy to forget. But I was wrong. There was no name calling, or derogatory messages on the voicemail. They were all pleasant, or empty with breathing and begging for me to give him a call. But I didn't call him. I went to see him.

I walked into his office and his head fell to the side. He looked up at me and smiled, holding his chin between his fingers, then sultrily parted his mouth to excuse one of his employees.

The gentleman left and he shut the door behind him. "You are a sight for sore eyes. I'm relieved you're okay. I must have left you a million messages." He hugged me.

"Yeah, about that…I'm sorry…I…"

"Don't apologize. I overstepped. But I don't regret it. I like you—a lot. And I'd do it again."

I pushed him away. "Therein lies the problem. I like you, too. But I love my husband, and I won't disrespect him any further."

"Look, I know I put you in an awkward position, but I am who I am. I wanted to kiss you and I did. I went for what I wanted, knowing I couldn't have it. And I still do. Even more so now in this moment." He stepped in closer.

I retreated to the window and he followed. "Lucas, I told you I'm not this person. I have wrestled with the guilt, and my part in all of this. I should have never called you, or allowed you to kiss me."

"Did you listen to my messages?"

"Yes." I sighed. "And I came here to apologize and tell you good-bye. Here's your phone."

He reached past the phone and caressed my wrist. "Keep it." He stuck it inside my coat pocket. "Since this is good-bye, can I have one final kiss?"

He grabbed my waist and pulled me away from the window, lowering his mouth to mine. He lifted my chin and kept his eyes open, planting his lips below my mouth, then to each of my cheeks.

I allowed him the pleasurable taste of my skin, granting him the request of one last kiss. It was soft, and gentle, and quick. I pulled back and he stole a second peck, speeding up the pace of my heart.

"Meeting you has changed me for the better," he said.

"I, too, have learned some things about myself since you came along."

"Like what?" he asked, seducing me with his eyes.

"That a rat has more than one hole to go to. And I'm not a rat."

An outburst of a chuckle moaned from his mouth. His hands fell to his side, and he watched me leave with a look of defeat written on his face. It was the look I aimed to remember of him. The face of what could have been my downfall. The face of temptation. The image of the disaster I would leave behind in New York, never knowing what would have been.

23

FEVER

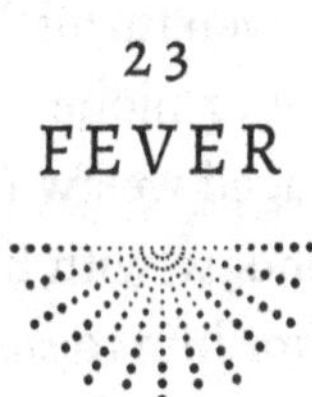

The trial and tribulation of my stay back in the states finally ended. I made peace with my mistakes, and prepared to return to the U.K., donating my belongings to a nearby shelter after the doorman took all he wanted once I departed the premises.

I tied up all of my loose ends except the delivery of Lucas's cell phone. Hours before the car arrived to drive me to the airport, I packaged it with a note inside, and sent it to his office by courier.

The packing, organizing, ripping and running took its toll on me. I lied in the bed, waiting for time to pass before my flight to Charlotte.

While studying the design in the ceiling, my mind wandered from one thing to the next. I imagined what Shannon would look like in her wedding dress, if she was going to be a bridezilla like Taylor, and how much Baby Tyler was going to look like Dylan.

A knock at the door startled me. It wasn't time to leave for the airport yet, so I peeped through the keyhole for a clue. "Oh God no," I said to myself, staring at Lucas in the hallway.

I invited him inside. He walked circles around my near empty living space.

I paced circles of my own across the slick floors. "How did you find me?"

He slid a finger between the curtains, then closed them back together. "All of these months I could have been here keeping you warm at night. I would have even furnished the place."

"I told you I don't need your money. I didn't need much for the short time I was here. I managed well with little."

He posed against the window with his back facing me. I stayed near the front door waiting for him to speak.

"I had to see you one more time," he said, walking towards me.

"But we already said our good-byes."

"I don't think we said them properly." He cornered me against the door.

He outlined his fingers across my lips slowly and delicately. I trembled with desire, no longer fighting the yearning of my pulsating southern urges. I opened my mouth slightly and panted as his fingertips parted my lips.

"Nadia, can I make love to you?"

"Yes please." I shuddered.

We kissed reverently, stripping away our layers, and dropping them on the floor as he mounted me on the bed. The aching and longing of him in my thoughts, would now become tangible as his rough, un-manicured hands squeezed my body beneath him.

"I don't want to be a good girl anymore." I confessed, looking directly in his eyes.

"Yes, you do." His deep voice whispered. "You'll be my good girl."

He sucked on my neck until the blood under my skin felt like it burst. I heaved at the sensation as he moved to the other side, then to my breasts where he tickled my nipples with his tongue, clenching them with his teeth.

The satiable manner of his technique delivered sensations instead of pain. "Be back in one sec," he whispered, sliding his head between my thighs where it belonged.

"Mmm." I moaned, thrusting my core upward while he fondled

my swollen lips with his, toying and tasting me. I jerked as my senses went wild with anticipation, then he licked my skin like an animal does when it's hungry. I cried out, "I can't take it anymore! I'm ready for you!"

He ignored my demand, caressing my ass while he fed from me, tongue twisting, and trilling my kitty as if he were rolling his r's in Spanish. I clung to the sheets as the vibrations paralyzed me. I could only lie there and wait for what was to come next. And I was not ready.

He penetrated the tip of his wood, but my rim fought his entry. "I promise I won't hurt you," he said, distracting me as he drilled his pipe inside.

I respired aloud to God while he stretched my walls. "Oh God!" I hollered.

"I knew you were holding heat." He growled in my ear, then gently bit my lobe. "Nadia." He purred. "I want you to look at me when you come."

I nodded okay, peeping at him through my lashes, witnessing the joy on his face for finally conquering me. He was a fiend atop of me, pressing his teeth firmly together, embracing me tightly so I couldn't escape. Relishing my nectar to the point I thought he would shed tears.

His hips swirled his manhood in and out of me so worthy I clenched his cock with my saturated treasure, making him woo and form a circle with his mouth. He lifted my legs and placed them above his shoulder.

I halted him, pressing my hands on his chest. "Lucas, I don't think I can handle you like this yet."

He stroked me once and I exhaled a sound of squeamish delight to his liking. So, he stroked again and again, faster and deeper. "Ahhh" I wailed, holding on to his shoulders with my eyes closed.

"Look at me." He ordered.

"I can't."

"Look at me, Love."

I opened my eyes as he demanded. He wiped the side of my face and swept my hair back, gazing at me without blinking and maintaining his rhythm. He ploughed and held his dick in place. I closed my eyes.

"No, my love. Look at me." He commanded.

I did as he wanted and looked at him while I climaxed, sounding off like a fire whistle. My mouth opened wide and he kissed me to muffle my roar. I could no longer obey his request and closed my eyes, digging my nails into his back. He orgasmed and rolled behind me, curling me into his arms, holding me close, and breathing heavily in my ear.

"He's not the only one who loves you." Lucas secured me into weakness and slumber.

A tapping noise woke me. I was still trapped in Lucas's arms. I wiggled my way free and looked on the floor to find the tapping noise. I saw nothing, then sat on the edge of the bed and held my face in my hands, covered in guilt, and confused by my actions.

I let out a sigh and heard the tapping sound again. I turned around to look back at Lucas sleeping peacefully in my bed, and choked on the air in my mouth.

Mash stood behind us, tapping his foot, and pointing a gun at Lucas. I waved my arms for him to put down the gun, incapable to form a word.

Mash wouldn't look at me. He stood there aiming at Lucas's back, zoned out in a rage.

My voice returned. "Mash don't do this. It's not worth it. Please put the gun down. Look at me please. I'm sorry. I don't know why I did this. It's my fault not his. Please, look at me."

His arm remained pointed at Lucas, but his eyes shifted to me. A tear dropped down each of his cheeks, and I fell to my knees, holding my naked body trying to cover myself.

Lucas woke up and called out for me. "Nadia. Nadia love, where are you?"

Mash's deep voice surprised him from behind. "Don't you dare say her name."

Lucas turned around and charged Mash from the bed.

I screamed. "No! Please stop! Both of you please stop!"

They ignored my cries and continued to tussle. The echo of the gun firing cut my ears.

I jumped up from the bed and held my chest. Thunderous knocking at the door woke me from my illicit dream. I peeped through the keyhole in fear my dream was about to become a reality, thankful to see the doorman standing on the opposite side.

"Your car has arrived ma'am. May I take your luggage?" he asked.

My blouse was wet with sweat, and my panties drenched from impure thoughts, but I still followed Paul downstairs, ready for a fresh start. I gave him the keys to the apartment, and we shook hands one final time as he opened the car door.

"Ms., Do you mind if I bum a ride with you?" Mash smiled at me from the front seat.

I stepped back on the curb. "I thought your flight was tomorrow?"

He hopped out and held me in his arms. "I changed it. I didn't want to wait another day to see you." He planted a wet one on me.

Inside the airport I grew nervous every time I saw a tall, slender, brown man walk near us in a navy coat. I breathed with relief when the wheels went up on the plane, happy the nightmare I had before the doorman woke me was in fact just a dream.

While overlooking the black ripples of waves below us, I vowed to forget Lucas existed, and to live with regret. Especially the regret of the words I wrote on the note inside the courier package I mailed to him.

'Leave this phone number in service.
It might ring one day.'

THE PLAYLIST

Thank you for diving into my fictional worlds. This Christmas my ensemble casts collide in a Mashup Novelette to celebrate love during the holidays. The On Track But Off Course Series meets The Hummus Series in, 'Levi & Launa Find Love'.

REVIEWS
ENCOURAGE
VORACIOUS
INTEREST
EVERY
WHERE TO
SUPPORT

ME, THE AUTHOR

I GREATLY APPRECIATE IT

XOXO

REVIEWS
ENCOURAGE
VORACIOUS
INTEREST
EVERY
WHERE TO
SUPPORT
ME, THE AUTHOR

T.K. RICHARDS is a multi-genre author of women's fiction and romance, featuring popular novels and novellas in Black Romance, Interracial/Multicultural Romance, Paranormal Romance, and YA Fiction. You can find her serialized fiction work on the Kindle Vella app. A graduate of Limestone University, T.K. has honors in Expository Writing, and was also the Poet Laureate of her graduating class. When she is not writing, she is immersed in the world of tennis, and binge watching movies—mostly comedy as she loves to laugh.

For more information about **T.K. Richards**, visit her website at www.tkrichards.com or subscribe to her newsletter at: https://tkrichardsnewsletter.ck.page

You can follow T.K. RICHARDS on the platforms listed below to interact with her personally:

facebook.com/Tkrichards

twitter.com/tkrichards1

instagram.com/t.k.richards

pinterest.com/TKWrites

tiktok.com/@tkrwrites

youtube.com/tkrichards

goodreads.com/T.k.richards

bookbub.com/authors/t-k-richards

amazon.com/author/Tkrichards

BY T.K. RICHARDS

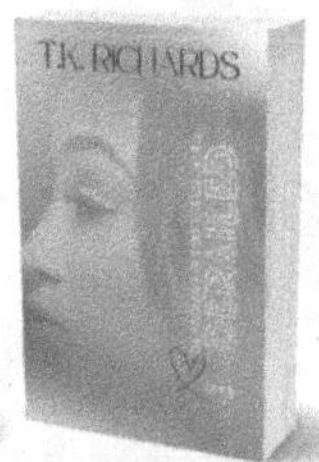
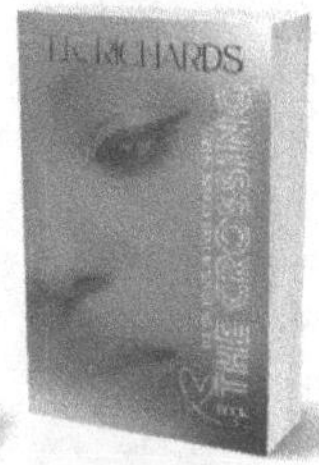